THE UNDEAD
DAY FIVE

RR HAYWOOD

Copyright © 2017 by RR Haywood

All rights reserved.

No part of this book may be reproduced in any form or by any electronic or mechanical means, including information storage and retrieval systems, without written permission from the author, except for the use of brief quotations in a book review.

Cover design and artwork by Eduardo Garay Arnaldos

❦ Created with Vellum

The Undead

DAY FIVE

rrhaywood.com

Chapter 1

Day Five

TUESDAY MORNING

FROM AN EMPTY WINDOW frame of an old cottage in the urban training zone, the infection watched as many hosts were torn down.

It saw the humans coming and sent the horde after them, but the daylight meant that it was slow and weak and couldn't respond fast enough; the infection feels each loss of each host and knows it is being diminished and reduced. It doesn't know how or why it came into existence, only that it is, and the primary function is to survive, and, if it must survive, then these losses must be stopped.

The infection recognises the humans that cause these problems. All over the world, the infection watches these humans fight back and inflict losses on its invaluable hosts, and it knows that it must stop this from happening, it must end the losses. In order to do this, it must evolve and learn how to fight back. The infection spread so rapidly that it knew it would only be a matter of a short time before it ruled this place and all in it. But it did not expect the ingenuity or bravery of these few humans. The masses were taken over within hours, but some were quick and fought back – or hid. The infection did not concern itself at first, knowing that the numbers it possessed would lead it to take them all, but now it senses there is a desperation to the situation. These humans are inflicting too many losses and this must be stopped. These potential hosts offering resistance are cunning and they use more than their bodies; they have tools and coordination. The infected host body stands still and watches as the recruits cut down the hosts; the brain inside the host is given more energy and synapses start flowing. The infection uses the intelligence and the memories stored inside this mind. But it doesn't understand these memories or thought processes, so it releases more energy and then feels as the host starts to take back control. The infection knows it can stop this at any time, so allows the host to exert that control. The infected body stares forward and then moves its eyes from left to right; the hands start clenching and unclenching and the rate of breathing increases. The energy flow is enhanced and control is given back to the host body, which falls to its knees screaming in agony, clutching its head at the intense pain surging from every cell. The body becomes demented and is raving in lunacy, staggering into walls and falling over furniture. The infection takes control and sends more energy into the nerve endings and the body screams with pain and drops to the floor, writhing in agony.

The infection sends more signals to the pain receptors and the host goes taut, the agony too much to bear. The body would normally shut down and slip into unconsciousness at this point, but the infection doesn't allow that, it keeps the body awake and learns as the electrical impulses are fired throughout the body. The mind has been given back, but the pain is so intense the host body stays rigid – hardly breathing – every vein sticks out and the muscles are tense and tight. Even death isn't an option now; death has happened once to this man and the infection will not allow that mercy now.

Slowly pulling back the flow of energy to the nerve ending and pain receptors, the infection diverts the energy to the parts of the brain that release endorphins and the pleasure receptors. The body slowly relaxes and the muscles release; the body twitches sporadically from the intense contractions of the muscles.

The body starts to smile and moan softly as it is flooded with chemicals, giving it an amazing feeling of warmth and security; then, as the pleasure heightens, there is a natural reaction from the body and, before long, its erection is straining against its trousers.

The Undead Day Five

The infection releases a surge of endorphins, and the body once again goes taut and the muscles contract as the feeling is too strong to bear. The infection eases the flow and draws back the control, piece by piece, testing and learning, as each function is given some power, then drawing it back to test other reactions. The body writhes in ecstasy, then eases back into a normal state. Then the body sits up and the knees bend to allow it to stand, but this is slow and cumbersome. The body puts its hands down to the floor and uses them to brace the weight as the body's feet find the balance needed.

The body slowly rises up into a standing position, then extends the arms out straight, then above the head. It bends the arms at the elbows and flexes them back out. It spins the arms round in circles, first forward and then backwards. The body jumps on the spot, heavy and unwieldy. Then another jump and the infection learns to control the flex of the tendons in the feet and toes to find balance. The body continues to jump and move about the room, the arms spinning and waving; it kneels down and jumps up, then takes small leaps forward and backwards. All across the world, various infected bodies go through the same moves, spinning and jumping. A release of energy to the nerve endings and all the bodies fall to the floor in agony. Endorphins are quickly released and the bodies stand up, drunkenly. In New York, Paris, Barcelona, Delhi, Singapore, and towns and cities all over the globe, the bodies work in the same pattern: leaping, running on the spot, dancing and weaving – as the infection fights to control the electrical impulses, watching through hundreds of host bodies' eyes, seeing different scenes but sharing the common feeling. While hundreds of thousands of host bodies across the world are cut down and slain by the brave people fighting back, the infection learns to control these few bodies.

While Howie and the recruits fought with grim determination, moving back a step at a time, the infected hosts were slaughtered – too slow and cumbersome, shambling and shuffling as the bullets ripped them apart. *Then, as night fell, the infection released the power that it had built up. It made the host bodies roar into the night, so they could find one another and send fear driving into the heart of the humans. The infected watched them run and hide and sent more hosts after them. The infection felt the church door starting to yield and knew it would be over within seconds; the smell of fear coming from inside was strong, but not as strong as it expected. Then it was over – and the hosts were torn apart* *and shredded by one man using a tool, and then the humans were together again – and it was done.*

The infection took the losses and learnt from them and watched from the upstairs window of the house in the urban training zone. It heard the men laugh and call to each other. It watched the man in the centre of the others be shown respect and deference. It heard the humans speak and the same word is repeated again and again. The infected body stands still now and stares out into the night. It watches as the sun rises and can feel its body slowing down to recover and repair.

The infection sends energy to the chest, makes air come out of the mouth, and moves the vocal chords to make sounds, such as it does when the darkness comes.

This time the noise is subtle and quiet. The body keeps practising, making noises, until it hears the word that sounds the same as the humans'. It repeats this word over and over again, drawing the sound out, until it resonates and becomes fluid. It is one word. It is: **Howie**.

Chapter 2

Through the night, the recruits sleep in the rear of the Saxon Armoured Personnel Carrier that is painted in the greys and blacks of urban camouflage.

Although exhausted to the point of near collapse, they still cleaned their weapons and made them ready before they slept. The sleeping bodies in the hot metal vehicle soon built up a high heat in the already warm and muggy night.

Dave had insisted that a look-out should be posted on the General Purpose Machine Gun at the top of the Saxon and, before long, recruits were falling out of the rear doors and sleeping directly on the ground underneath the vehicle, just to escape the heat. Howie slept in the front and had woken mid-way through the night to find Jamie Reese on lookout duty. He could see that Reese was wilting and fighting sleep, so Howie relieved him and took over the GPMG.

Howie felt the heat in the vehicle as he climbed into the rear to go up through the sentry hole, and he opened the doors to let some air in. He roused some of the sleeping men and told them to sleep outside. The recruits were sweating profusely, but were so exhausted they just slept on until he poked and prodded them and half-dragged them out into the cooler air, fearing they would become dehydrated.

Dave roused and saw what was happening; he nodded to Howie to show he understood and then climbed out of the front cabin and onto the top of the vehicle and lay down on his back, asleep within seconds.

Howie watched from the sentry point, turning around slowly and making use of a high-powered light that was connected by a lead to a power supply within the Saxon. As he watched, he thought of his mother and father and the sacrifice they must have made trying to come for him. He had no evidence of their demise, and his greatest fear was that he would see them as zombies and either have to destroy them or be eaten by them. They might still be alive, but Howie knew this was very unlikely. The only family he had left was his sister, Sarah, living in London. Howie's parents had left him a note, saying that they had spoken to Sarah and she was safe in her apartment. The last four days had been spent trying to get to London to rescue Sarah; his home town was gone and so were all the other places he had seen so far. A message he had heard from a radio broadcast had told any survivors to head for the Forts on the South Coast, and to stay away from London.

He'd known that getting through London would be impossible without some serious assistance, so he and Dave had travelled to Salisbury to find something big, heavy, and armoured to get through the massed hordes that must be waiting there. There was no way of contacting Sarah and telling her to sit tight and wait; he could only hope she was being smart and staying hidden.

Howie looked down at the recruits sleeping; thinking of them as recruits made him smile a little. They were just boys, really, none of them older than eighteen, and they had been sent to join the Territorial Army by a new government scheme to give young unemployed people some experience of life and instil discipline in them. Thirty lads had only just arrived at Salisbury Army Centre on Friday, when the outbreak started; they'd been excited and full of anticipation. Now there were only nine left, and they were willing to listen and learn from Dave.

The Undead Day Five

None of them had to go with Howie and Dave to London, but they knew that by staying together, they had a greater chance of survival.

A groaning noise alerted Howie and he tuned in, listening intently into the night. He flicked the high-powered flashlight on and swept it around in a slow arc. A zombie was crawling towards them. Howie aimed the GPMG then paused, knowing that the noise would wake them all up and possibly draw more of the undead to them. Howie clambered up through the hole and dropped down to the ground. He then reached into the cabin and pulled out his beloved axe, walking slowly to the zombie. The undead was crawling pitifully slowly and his legs looked mangled and crushed, but still he worked his way forward, groaning with anticipation at the thought of biting into new flesh.

Howie crouched down, off to the side, and watched the zombie turn and start towards him. The flesh on the face and arms was very grey with a sickening pallor, the stench of rotting flesh oozed off the zombie and made Howie pull his head back in disgust. The eyes were still red and bloodshot, and Howie noticed that the hands were cut down to the bones from having to drag itself along the rough ground.

Howie stood up and shook his head at the disgusting creature. He took the axe and stepped forward, raising it high and then sweeping it down directly onto the neck to remove the head. As the axe flew through the air, the zombie looked at Howie and made a sound that terrified him.

Howie jumped back with a shout as the axe struck, missing the neck and cleaving into the head. He dropped the axe and fell back onto the ground, sitting still and staring at the now dead undead.

Dave came running up and looked down at the cadaver, and then at Howie.

'He said … my name,' Howie stammered.

Chapter 3

Sarah wakes up slowly as the bright sunlight streams through the smart black blinds covering her bedroom window.

Dust particles dance and shimmer in the air from her soft breath.

Long, dark strands of hair spread out across the expensive silk sheets of the king-sized double bed.

Sarah sits up slowly and looks at her reflection in the mirrored doors of the built-in wardrobes. She looks intently, with a look of concentrated determination which slowly morphs into sadness. With a long sigh, she shimmies over the bed and stands up, stretching her arms and legs out. Sarah then walks into the en-suite bathroom and reaches for the light switch, but the electricity went out a couple of days ago and she curses herself for forgetting.

She checks the cold water tap and is pleasantly surprised that clear water still gushes out. She starts to brush her teeth and looks longingly at the large glass-sided shower cubicle in the middle of the room, then sniffs at her armpits and pulls her head away from the stale smell of body odour.

There are pans and pots on every surface; each filled with water and covered with cling film and aluminium foil. Sarah knew that once the electricity went out she would have to preserve her supplies, so quickly filled every available receptacle from her small apartment. Even the kitchen sink is full of clean water, and she hasn't flushed the toilet for a couple of days now. The warm weather has meant that she's been sweating lightly nearly all the time, especially at night when the air is so still and hot. Her tight black vest top clings to her body from moisture. Sarah has been washing with cotton cloths and only using the water sparingly, but now, after several days, she longs for a shower. The air is so warm and humid and she can just imagine the cold water spraying onto her sticky body.

'Sod it,' she says to herself and quickly strips her clothes off, leaving them in a pile on the floor.

Naked, she steps into the cubicle and turns the dial; a powerful jet of freezing water pummels into her skin, taking her breath away and making her squeal. The cold water is pleasant torture and she soaks herself, watching as goose pimples come up on her arms and legs. She quickly scrubs her body with soap and washes her hair, turning the shower off as the last of the bubbles are rinsed away. She steps out and takes the thick cotton towel hanging from a hook; she walks back in front of the bathroom mirror and stands naked, holding the towel down at her side, enjoying the feeling of the warm air drying her wet skin.

After a few minutes, she is dressed in jeans and a baggy t-shirt and finally goes into the lounge area – a small room with a kitchenette on one end. The apartment was subsidized by her employer, one of the perks of working for a large, corporate bank. The downside was that she had to respond to work whenever she was called, and that was quite often during the recession. But even a tiny apartment like hers, in a swish block, would cost a fortune – far more than she could ever afford.

Sarah finally plucks up the courage and steps to the large windows, pulling the blinds up. She slides back the single patio door, steps out onto the tiny balcony that overlooks most of Central London, and glances down onto the streets below. Her heart sinks as she sees the thousands and thousands of zombies crammed into the streets. Even the road is not visible, because they are so densely packed. The only times she has seen crowds like this are for huge Royal Weddings or the London Marathon.

But these aren't crowds waiting for a glimpse of someone famous; these are hordes of rotting, dirty, filthy zombies that want to eat human flesh. Sarah shudders and steps back inside. She closes the door but then opens it slightly, in defiance. They are down there and, as far as she is aware, they haven't tried to climb up to her, and the apartment needs fresh air. She walks over to the fridge, and again forgets that the power is gone. It is now empty as she has eaten all of the perishable food and is now on to the tinned goods.

'Sod it,' she says again and steps over to the wall cupboard; she closes her eyes and reaches in. She knows there are some tinned goods inside and she has been making herself select them at random so that she doesn't just eat the nicer things first.

She feels for a tin and quickly pulls it out, holding it in front of her face as she slowly opens her eyes and peeks down at the tin of … tuna.

'Sod it.'

She opens the tin, takes a fork, and sits down on the sofa to slowly munch through the dry fish. Giving up within two mouthfuls and going back to the cupboard, she mooches through the various bottles of sauces and condiments, deciding on an almost empty bottle of barbeque sauce. She shakes the thick liquid down to the cap end before squirting it over the rest of the tuna and mixing it in. She starts eating again, and whilst doing so, her mind travels back to Friday.

A trendy wine bar was what Howie would call it, and Sarah smiles at the memory of her brother making jokes about her whole life being '… a trendy gym, a trendy apartment, and a trendy social life.' Sarah knew, though, that success in her line of work depended on being able to socialise, or network. So she made contacts within all of the communities of the financial district.

Friday evening was the same as any other: calls were made, emails sent, text messages put out, and the *in crowd* descended into

Central London for drinks and Tapas at Charlie's, which was owned and ran by the sleazy Charlie himself. He was always trying it on with the female staff and customers, despite his wife working there. Tapas was appointed with sleek black minimalist furniture and exposed wooden flooring, and photos of pebbles and stones in various poses finished the scene; Sarah knew that it was stomach-churning, fake, and contrived, but business was business and it had to be done. So she laughed at the right times and gradually made her way through the crowds with her colleagues. A simple black evening dress was all that she wore; simple, elegant, and classic was how her close friends said she looked – which was exactly the look that she aimed for. Too many of the female financiers showed way too much flesh out of the office and it just didn't feel appropriate to her. Her dad had always said: '… if you want to be taken seriously, you have to act seriously.' And his words had stuck throughout her short career.

Younger than Howie by two years, she had moved to London at the tender age of twenty-three and had been here for two years now. The shine of the city had already worn off, and Sarah knew it wouldn't be long before she wanted out of it. Sarah had seen the desperation of the older people, clinging to their power and fortunes and trying to stay with the in crowd all of the time; this just made her sad and more resolved to get out when she could.

Smoking had saved her life – it's not often that people can say that.

Sarah had been addicted for years, and controlled the habit by having the odd couple of cigarettes at lunchtime and then after work; so many of the young financiers were health freaks – using the companies' gyms and clubs during lunch hours or after work. They called it '… having a sesh.' Sarah was amazed at how many of them used cocaine and did so in public, but would then shun the smokers, calling their habit dirty and cancerous.

Taking the opportunity to nip outside, and just managing to avoid the grope being offered by Charlie, she talked with her co-conspirator and smoking colleague, Lisa. They chatted as they walked around the side of the building into a quieter side street and both lit up, giggling like schoolgirls, inhaling the smoke and relaxing with idle gossip.

'Well, that Jonathon tried it on with me last night, I just knew he would, the dirty bugger,' Lisa said.

'He did? What did you do?' Sarah replied.

'What do you think I did? I told him that I'm a strict Catholic girl and he should bugger off!' Lisa said in a very serious tone, then cackled evilly.

'Oh, you didn't – you naughty girl,' Sarah laughed, waiting for the juicy details of the illicit encounter. A scream came from the front of the trendy wine bar, and it made them both jump; they darted forward to look around the edge of the building. They were just in time to see Charlie standing there in his expensive designer jeans, brown boots, and tucked-in black shirt – with his podgy stomach pushing against the material.

A very pretty girl with long, blonde hair was shouting loudly at him as he backed away with his hands raised up in front of him, palms facing her, acquiescent and trying to *shush* her.

'YOU FILTHY BASTARD, YOU GRABBED MY ARSE!' the woman screamed at Charlie, then slapped him hard across the face, causing his perfectly-styled messy hair to get dishevelled. Charlie backed away and begged the woman to keep her voice down. She became angrier and started throwing more haymakers at him. One of the large bouncers stepped forward and restrained the woman, pulling her back.

'YOU CRAZY BITCH!' Charlie shouted, and ordered the bouncer to take her down the street.

'He had that coming, the sleazy pig,' Sarah said.

'Oh, he's disgusting – he's always grabbing my arse and trying to squeeze my tits,' replied Lisa.

'I don't know why we keep coming here, it's always the same people and the same thing, and that dirty sleazebag trying to grope anything that moves; he's a sex pest,' Sarah said.

'You know what I heard, he just got back from his brother's wedding in Greece where he got off with the bride's best mate, and now he keeps going down to see her, right under his poor wife's nose,' Lisa said.

'Someone should report him to the police, that's got to be sexual assault or something,' Sarah said.

'Oh ... hang on, it's not quite over yet.'

A well-built man with a bald head came storming up the street, straight towards Charlie who was now talking to his two bouncers. As the man got closer, he pointed directly at Charlie.

'Did you grab my girlfriend's arse? You dirty fucker,' the man shouts as he gets closer.

Charlie quickly starts stepping back, hiding behind his bouncers. One of them moves forward and extends an arm out to the man; a clear warning to stay back. The man knocks it out of the way and quickly punches the bouncer in the face, causing him to fly back and knock Charlie into a set of tables, upsetting the drinks all over the nearest customers. The second bouncer moves in to grab the angry man but gets head butted and sent flying too. Charlie is on his feet and moving backwards, away from the angry man.

'Please mate, take it easy, calm down, I didn't do anything, it's all a misunderstanding,' Charlie pleads, seeing his two bouncers down on the ground, clutching at their faces. Sarah and Lisa are laughing hard, watching Charlie beg the man to stop whilst backing away into more tables and knocking drinks over. The bald man lunges at Charlie and grabs him by the front of his shirt, then throws him down onto the floor. Sarah, Lisa, and a half-dozen other previously-groped women all cheer at the sight of the sex pest getting his just rewards. The angry man glances around at the sound of cheering and smiles awkwardly at first, confused about the reaction. One woman shouts out to cheers and whistles:

'Go on then, have him – he's grabbed all of us, the dirty beast.'

The bald man smiles at the women and bows his head before walking intently towards Charlie, who is scurrying away on his backside, one hand up in the air, still trying to defuse the situation.

'Please mate, I didn't do anything, you touch me and I'll get the law on you, there's CCTV here.' The man bends down and pulls

Charlie to his feet by the front of his clothes and punches him once in the face.

The women erupt in cheers and start applauding. People pile out of the main door to watch the action and more join in by clapping. The man hits him again in the face and the crowd cheer even louder. Someone shouts 'TWO' and the man pounds him again. The crowd shouts 'THREE.'

The man isn't hitting him hard, but hard enough to stun Charlie and humiliate him. The bouncers are back on their feet now and are starting forward to help their boss. A woman steps out from the crowd and stands in front of them.

'DON'T DO NOTHING – HE GOT THIS COMING!' the woman shouts at the bouncers in a strong Eastern European accent.

'That's the wife then,' Lisa laughs as the crowd shouts 'FOUR!' A loud shout erupts from over the road and Sarah looks over to see another fight taking place.

'Jesus, this place is getting worse, look at them going for it.'

Lisa stares over and they both watch as a man is being attacked on the ground by another man. Some other people run over and start to pull the man away by grabbing at his shoulders and body. The man is thrashing about and appears to be trying to force his face into the other man's neck. The attacker then springs up and launches himself at one of the rescuers.

'Oh my God, did you see that?' Sarah asks.

'Yeah, that's awful,' Lisa replies. There is a big ruckus going on now across the road as more people try to subdue the crazy man. He refuses to stop and keeps lunging his head at more people, biting them and causing them to jump backwards. The man who was on the floor sits up after a few minutes and slowly looks around.

'At least he's all right, I thought he was dead,' Lisa said. The man gets to his feet and suddenly lunges forward and bites into the neck of another man. Screams and shouts erupt and the bald man, holding the now bloodied Charlie, stops pounding and looks over at the mass brawl taking place. He lets Charlie go, who slumps to the ground whimpering. The crowd are all silent now.

Some people are running into the melee, and some are trying to escape. One woman, dressed in a smart, black business suit staggers out of the confusion, clutching her neck, blood spurting out between her fingers. She staggers across the road and falls, and the bald man tries to catch her and lower her gently to the ground. The man shouts for something to stop the bleeding and presses his already bloody hands into the side of her neck.

Women are screaming and men are running about in panic. The fighting gets worse and more people get involved, until nearly the whole street is brawling.

Sarah starts to take in some of the details; despite not being experienced in street fights, even *she* understands that biting is not a normal action.

'We should get out of here,' Lisa murmurs to Sarah.

'What? Christ, yes, let's go,' Sarah responds, shaking herself. Sarah and Lisa start down the main road, but quickly see that the road ahead is also blocked by people fighting. They turn round and try to go the other way, but that too is blocked.

'What the fuck is going on?' Lisa shouts.

'I don't know ... quick, down here.' Sarah grabs her hand and they start back towards the entrance to the side street that they were smoking in, just a few minutes ago. They pass the front of Tapas again and Lisa screams as she sees the bald man being pulled down by the woman in the smart business suit.

The woman is biting into his neck, gouging the flesh away, and hot crimson blood is pouring down her face. They scurry past and enter the darkness of the quiet street. Both stop halfway down to take off their high heels and run in bare feet. They burst out of the street into another main road, also swamped with cafés, restaurants, and wine bars, and hundreds of screaming people covered in blood and clutching facial and body wounds. Sarah and Lisa run down the pavement, dodging around people fighting. Blood spurts out from an arterial bleed, soaking Lisa on her face and bare arms. They continue to run, narrowly missing being attacked by inches. Within a short distance, they reach Sarah's apartment block.

'Come in with me, Lisa – you can't stay out here on your own,' Sarah says, panting heavily.

'I can't Sarah, I've got to get home!' Lisa breaks away and starts running down the street.

'I'll call you when I'm home,' she yells. Sarah watches her run, then turns to go into her own block, but movement to her left catches her eye and she sees a man staggering into view. His shirt is blood-soaked and half his face is torn away. He sees Sarah and starts directly towards her. Sarah fumbles at the numbers on the key-coded entrance lock. Her fingers move too fast and she has to press clear and start again. Finally, she pushes through the door and slams it shut behind her.

In the foyer, Sarah presses the button to call the lift. While waiting, she peers at the front door and watches the man through the glass, staggering past the door – then he stops and walks towards the plate glass.

Sarah pulls back and urges the lift to move faster. The doors open with a loud ping and Sarah gets inside and waits for the slow climb to her floor. She doesn't hear or see anyone else, and gets safely into her flat.

She then pulls her mobile phone out of her bag and curses that she forgot it was on silent. The screen flashes with missed calls from HOME. Her parents have been calling her again and again. She presses the phone and waits for the connection. Her dad answers and lets out a loud sigh.

'Sarah, thank God you're okay,' he says.

'Dad, what's happening, there's loads of fighting and people being attacked and a man had his face hanging off,' Sarah babbles into the phone.

'Sarah, listen to me. The phones will be down soon, something bad is happening everywhere. I don't know what it is but you stay in your flat, okay? You must lock yourself in and wait for us.' Howard speaks slowly and firmly, making sure she takes it all in.

'Dad, what? What's going on, are you and Mum okay?'

'We're fine, Sarah, your mother's right here. We are going to get Howie and then we'll come and get you, wait there – do not go out or leave the flat.'

'Is Howie okay, Dad? Is this everywhere? I've been out in town and it was awful.'

'Yes, Sarah – it's everywhere, now you must stay there ...' The line goes dead.

Sarah panics and yells into the phone, over and over again:
'DAD!'

She presses the END CALL button and tries to call them back. She keeps trying again and again, then calls Howie but gets no tone and then she works her way through her call list one by one.

All around the world, people screamed into their phones, desperately trying to make contact with their loved ones. The huge numbers crashed the networks and the engineers were busy fighting for their lives, like everyone else, and couldn't bring the systems back online.

Sarah had never had a landline connected; the mobile signal in most of Central London was always brilliant and the building provided secure wireless connection.

Sarah tried using her computer, but the Internet was down too. After hours of frantic calling and texting, she gave up and sank onto the sofa, curling up and sobbing. After some time, she remembered the television; she had rarely watched any TV. Sarah flicked through the channels, but each one was either blank or showing a static image apologising for the loss in broadcast.

Those were the events of Friday. Now it's Tuesday and there is still no sign of her family.

Sarah finishes the tuna and discards the empty can into the waste bin. She is feeling a little stir crazy and yesterday sneaked out to knock on her neighbours' doors – but there was no reply and she ran back inside her own apartment.

She knows that she has to keep mentally alert and that regular physical exercise releases endorphins into the system. She grabs her *iPod* and changes into a pair of shorts and a sporty vest top. Naturally very slim and lithe, regular workouts in the company gym helped keep her fit and toned. Selecting her gym play list, Sarah commenced exercising, again cursing herself that she had the shower first instead of waiting.

For the next two hours, Sarah punishes herself with hard physical exertion: running fast on the spot, then doing star jumps, squat thrusts, push ups, and sit ups; then she makes use of the kitchen worktop for dips. Loud dance and rock music blare directly into her inner ear, pushing her to work harder and faster. Eventually, she flakes out, crashing down to the floor, gulping air down and pulling the small white speakers out of her ears.

As she recovers, she tries to think how many apartments there are in the building. There are many floors, maybe twenty or twenty-five, and most of the apartments are small so the developers could make more money.

So... maybe four apartments per floor – apart from the big, luxury ones at the top – that would make it around one hundred apartments in my block. There must be someone else alive in this building and there should be a decent amount of water storage to supply the apartments. Which must mean there is plenty of water – so ... I can have another shower!

Sarah runs for the bathroom before she allows any doubt to creep in. Again, having showered under the pleasantly cold water, she gets dressed and makes her mind up – she is going to go out of her apartment and see if anyone else is still here. What harm can it do? Sarah selects a large knife from the kitchen drawer and starts towards the front door.

'Sod it,' she exclaims, as she slowly opens her front door.

Chapter 4

'Oh ... who did that?' Alex exclaims.

'Cookey' Cooke bursts out from underneath the Saxon, clutching his nose.

'Tucker, was that you? Stinky fucker!' Cookey shouts back, after taking a few steps away. Tucker chuckles to himself and then lets rip with another loud fart, causing more of the recruits to burst away from the rear of the vehicle.

'You dirty fucker,' Darren Smith yells, as Tucker carries on laughing.

I start giggling myself from my spot at the top of the Saxon vehicle. Dave took the last look-out during the night, and I got another couple of hours' sleep before the sun finally came up.

'What time is it?' Nicholas Hewitt stands and stretches out.

'Just gone 6 a.m.,' I say, out loud, so they can all hear.

'You lot feeling any better today?' I get a mixed response.

'Right, we need to make a move. Load up and we'll go back to the main buildings and find some food.'

'Hang on, I need a piss,' Simon Blowers calls out, and runs out from the Saxon, stopping after a few metres and relieving himself onto the grass.

Within minutes, he is joined by all of us, in a row, pissing in the warm summer morning; contented sighs and long groans sound out as bladders are relieved.

'I'm bloody starving,' Tucker says.

'No surprise there then,' Cookey says to a cackle of laughter.

'Stop talking about food, I feel like my throat's been cut,' Curtis Graves says.

'What? You didn't even do anything last night Gravesy – you were pissing about, driving that *Land* Rover all night, while we were fighting for our lives,' one of them shouts, and then they are off again, bantering and jibing.

We slowly load back into the Saxon and I take the driver's seat. The Bedford 500 6-cylinder engine roars to life, and I engage the first gear and pull away. The Saxon is a big, squat-looking thing with massive tyres and can hold up to ten soldiers in the rear. From looking at the controls I can see it has 2-wheel and 4-wheel drive capability, but I leave it in normal at the moment.

The ground is hard and compacted from the scorching hot summer, and the Saxon makes light work of it until we reach the smooth surface of the road that leads back into the main area. I familiarise myself with the vehicle while we go over the low bumps, causing the lads in the back to bounce around. I think back to the night before, when the zombie said my name. I theorise that it must have been just the body expelling air, and in the eerie night my imagination made it sound like my name.

'You all right mate?' I say to Dave.

He is sitting in the passenger seat of the cabin.

'Yes, Mr. Howie,' he replies, deadpan as normal.

'You hungry too, mate? I'm famished.'

'Yes.'

'So, what do we need to do? Get some food and go to the armoury ... anything else?'

'I don't think so; more ammunition and a bit more kit from the stores would be good.'

'Okay mate, food first though – we could split up and use the

The Undead Day Five

two teams we had yesterday, one for cooking and one for getting the stuff, with you.'

'Okay, Mr. Howie.'

I'm sure most of the lads are doing the same as me and thinking only of food and their stomachs. We follow the road for several miles; the plains are massive and stretch out on either side as far as the eye can see. Eventually, we drive into the main building area. There are undead bodies littering the ground everywhere. Flies and insects are buzzing between the cadavers and I realise just how much of a disease risk all of the corpses across the country are.

'Right, everyone out,' I call, as I bring the vehicle to a stop on the large parade square.

'We will split into two teams. Tucker, you're on team Alpha, aren't you?'

'Yes, Sir,' he replies, but looks worried.

'Team Alpha will come with me and get the grub ready. Team Bravo are going with Dave to get what he needs from the stores and the armoury. Right, who knows where the … food place is?'

'It's called the Mess, sir and it's over here.' Tucker starts off immediately, followed by the members of our team.

'STOP RIGHT THERE!' Dave bellows out in his drill sergeant voice, and everyone freezes, including me. I look around quickly, trying to identify the threat; my assault rifle already raised up. I see Blowers and Cookey are doing the same.

'WHERE ARE YOUR WEAPONS?' Dave shouts, and I realise that half the recruits have got out and started moving off, their rifles still in the Saxon.

'GET YOUR WEAPONS AND KEEP THEM WITH YOU AT ALL TIMES!' Dave's voice does the trick and they scramble back to the Saxon and gather their weapons, looking sheepish and embarrassed. I nod at Dave and he nods back.

'See you in a bit, mate – say an hour? Will that be long enough?'

'Yes, Mr. Howie.'

We set off to the 'Mess', and I wonder why the Army has to have such weird names for everything.

The Mess looks like most of the other buildings from the outside. The door leads into a corridor, which opens into a large canteen-style dining room with long tables and benches. There is a long serving counter at one end; hot plates and cold cabinets are dark and cold.

Tucker walks down the room, rubbing his hands.

'I don't know what they'll have left; I guess the meat might be off by now. What day is it? Tuesday? We'll see, there might be something decent we can use – I'll go and have a look.' He's in his element now – he is the official cook and food supplier for our band of misfits. I follow Tucker into the kitchen area, which is spotless and very modern-looking: huge ovens, multiple sinks, and various equipment are around the sides. There are lots of work surfaces in the middle. Tucker walks through, taking it all in.

'Have you done cooking before then, Tucker?' I ask him.

'I was joining the Catering Corps, sir. I love food and always have done loads of cooking, as you can probably tell,' he jiggles his large belly and laughs.

'Ah, here we are ...' He opens two large, metal doors that lead into a huge walk-in chill room.

'Won't all that be off now, mate? If the power's been off for a few days,' I ask, and follow him inside.

'The Army uses a different power supply to the normal grid, it's gone now, but I was hoping it stayed on long enough to keep this lot chilled. Plus these are very well insulated from the heat outside, so it takes a while for the temperature to rise.'

I see what he means; although the power is definitely out, the chilled room is decidedly colder than the kitchen or the outside.

'Now let's see, they must use the LILO method – so we just need to work out where that starts ...' Tucker says as he starts rummaging through boxes and packets.

'The what, mate?' I ask him.

'The LILO method means Last In Last Out. Which means they have a system to see when the freshest stock is added, so they use the oldest stock first.'

'Ah, I see, that makes sense.'

Tucker identifies the freshest line and starts pulling boxes out into the kitchen. I call the rest of the lads and we start a chain, piling it up on the work surfaces, until there is a considerable mound. I start poking through and see boxes of red meat, beef, and whole chickens. I smell each of them in turn but they all seem quite fresh. Tucker walks back into the kitchen as I'm sniffing.

'They must have had a delivery of new produce on Friday, so we're lucky this lot is still good,' he says.

'Are you using all of it?' I ask him, surprised at the pile of goods.

'Might as well, it will only go bad otherwise.' He stops and stares at the pile and immediately starts separating them.

Tucker is, by far, the least fit of the recruits, and he gets a lot of stick for it, but watching him now, he looks focussed and very happy.

'Anything we can do, mate?' Roland McKinney asks Tucker.

'Oh yes, the power is still on ...' Tucker exclaims as he turns a dial on one of the gas hobs. Then he checks if the oven is working.

'Right, Roland, can you grab some of those pans and fill them with water? Darren ... if you start cutting these up into small chunks,' Tucker thrusts a box at Darren and moves on to Nicholas Hewitt.

'Nick, could you start chopping the veg, please, mate.'

'Anything I can do, Tucker?' I ask him.

'Err ... no, sir – thanks anyway – but we can manage.'

I leave them to it and make my back out of the building and across to the parade square. The Saxon looks massive; it must be over two-and-a-half metres in height and over five metres in length. I feel more optimistic about our chances of getting through London but, again, the delay concerns me. These lads didn't have to come with us into the plains yesterday. I know they said that sticking together increases the chances of survival, but getting that Saxon was my objective and I did it to rescue my sister. I put them in danger for my own ends. In the church when the ammunition ran low and we were seconds from being invaded, not one of them moaned or said a word, but they stood together and prepared for the worst. So ... the least I can do now is give them some time for food and rest. I meet Dave at the Saxon and we watch the recruits bringing boxes of ammunition out. Dave takes the magazines out and stows them in compartments in the vehicle. Then he does the same with the spare rifles and ammunition for the GPMG – then more clothing – and finally some NATO helmets.

Once loaded, we head over to the Mess and walk in to a wonderful aroma: a mixture of meats and sauces that sets my mouth watering at once. Tucker has done an amazing job. There are bowls and trays of food in the middle of one of the tables.

A few minutes later and we are all tucking in, piling plates with food and shovelling it in to our mouths without manners or etiquette.

There are laughs and jokes around the table as everyone eats their fill.

Dave stays quiet and eats an enormous amount of food for such a slightly-built man. We sit back, relaxed and contented, and drink strong coffee.

'So, I'm going to head to London with Dave. I promised I would drop some of you off on the way ...' I let the question hang in the air.

'Sir, if it's all right with you, I'd rather stick with you two until you get to the Forts. I haven't really got anywhere else to go,' Blowers speaks first, his voice steady and decisive.

'Yes, mate, of course – but going to London is going to be hard – are you sure this is what you want to do?'

'Yes, Sir. I think Cookey feels the same way, we talked about it earlier.' Blowers looks to Cookey who nods in affirmation.

'I won't last five minutes on my own and besides, someone has to do the food and make the brews,' Tucker offers.

'That's great mate, thank you,' I say to Tucker. 'McKinney, what about you, mate?'

'Well ... I want to see my family, but I know they would have headed with everyone to the Forts ... if they haven't ...'

'I understand,' I interject, to try and save him the hardship of having to say it.

'But, there's no point me trying for home on my own – especially after seeing what they are like at night. So, if it's okay, I want

The Undead Day Five

to come with you too.' McKinney looks down at his empty plate, clearly uncomfortable with feeling like he has to ask.

'Lads, Dave and I would be more than happy to take you all with us, you've proved yourself. Trust me, it's not me doing you a favour, it's the other way 'round.'

'I'm going to head off, sir – if that's all right,' Alan Booker offers suddenly.

'No problem Alan, where you heading to?' I ask him.

'I'll try home first and then the Forts, if that fails. I live in the other direction – so I'll find something to take, save you having to drive away from your direction.'

'Alan, after what you've done for us mate, it's really not an issue if you need a ride somewhere,' I say to him.

'Nah, thanks anyway. I can take something to use,' he says, but looks sheepish and avoids eye contact.

'How will you take something, Alan? Even Dave and I struggled to find transport at times. It's not as easy as you would think.'

'Nah … it will be okay. I sort of know how to take cars without keys – if you get my meaning.'

'Ah … a misspent youth eh, mate? Well, it's a pity to lose you. Feel free to change your mind.'

'Thanks, Mr. Howie. I really appreciate it.' Alan is the only one that wants to leave. The others try and convince him to stay, but I can see his mind is made up.

Half an hour later, we are driving out of the gates and down the road.

Alan insists on being dropped off at the main junction and he gets out with his rifle, ammunition, and rucksack. There's a silence after he goes and we drive on quietly. The recruits have been through so much together, in such a short space of time, and the loss hits them hard.

Cookey makes an effort to crack a joke, but it falls flat.

'Now … are the rest of you sure that you want to come with us?' I shout back to the lads. 'Because there's going to be a lot of zombie mother fuckers that need killing. Dave and I did want to keep them to ourselves, but seeing as you lot have helped out, we are willing to share them – but not if you're going to be holding back.'

A few muttered responses.

'Oh yes, a whole lot of zombies that want to eat brains …' a few chuckles this time.

'BRAINS … I MUST HAVE THEM BRAINSSSS …' I groan the words out and then look across at Dave.

'EAT DAVE'S BRAIIINNNSSS …' A few more laughs, especially when Dave looks at me with his usual deadpan expression.

'COOKEY NO HAVE ANY BRAAAINS TO EAT THOUGH …' They laugh properly this time and start ripping on Cookey, who takes it well and abuses them back.

The tension is broken, for a little while, at least.

Chapter 5

Sarah treads softy down the carpeted hallway, creeping forward and stopping at the first door. She knocks gently and listens with her ear pressed to the door and, after a few seconds of silence, she tries the door handle and is not surprised to find that the door is locked. She moves down the corridor, checking each door, knocking and listening and then slowly pushing the door handle down. Sarah hasn't heard any noise from the neighbouring flats since the *event* began, which is unusual because she can normally hear the muted tones of the televisions, music being played, or the tones of voices.

She realises that she has never heard anyone from above or below her apartment, so has nothing to gauge whether the occupiers will still be there. Her floor is finished quickly; there is no noise and all of the doors are locked. Out of habit, she moves towards the lift doors and goes to press the CALL button, only remembering, at the last second, that the power is out. She moves to the fire door and slowly pushes it open, looking down into the stairwell. The apartment block is modern and finished to a high standard; the developer went to the extent of carpeting the emergency stairwell and having brass rails fitted.

Some of the more health-conscious residents used the stairs for a daily workout. The carpet is light brown, carefully selected to absorb moisture and street dirt from the boots of delivery drivers. The developer also thought to add glass panes to each fire door so that natural light filters into the stairwell.

'Up or down?' Sarah whispers to herself.

Living on the 14th floor meant she was just over halfway up. She stands still for some minutes, considering which way to go. In the end, she chooses to go up, knowing it will be quicker for her to run back down the stairs if she has to escape anything. The memories of seeing the undead bite into the living makes her shiver with fear as she starts to ascend the stairs, keeping to the central carpeted section to deaden her footfalls.

There are two sets of stairs between each floor, and she is at the next landing door very quickly, crouching behind the door and listening, then raising herself up slowly to peer through the glass pane and out into the corridor. The view is exactly the same as her floor: carpeted corridor with four apartments, two on each side, and a large picture window at the end. She creeps out until she is through the doorway and gently closes the door behind her. She repeats the actions from her floor, moving from door to door. Each apartment is quiet and the silence only serves to add to the tension and fear she is feeling. She moves stealthily back to the stairwell and climbs up to the 16th floor.

By the 19th floor she is more nonchalant, and the knife is held down at her side, rather than up and ready. She still tries the handles but her movements become less stealthy and covert and she spends less time at each door. By the 20th floor the knife is in her back pocket, and she walks normally down the corridor and knocks loudly at each door before trying the door handle, not bothering to listen this time.

Thinking that there is clearly no one there – the whole block must be empty – she makes her way back down the corridor and into the stairwell.

Up the stairs and onto the 21st floor. Again she knocks and tries each door handle – but there is no sign of life.

The Undead Day Five

'Where is everyone?' she mutters. She goes back into the stairwell and climbs further up, her thigh muscles still aching from the two hours of exercise.

Feeling hot, thirsty, and sweaty, she reaches the 21st floor and pushes the door open before stepping into the corridor.

Thinking of a cold drink and another cold shower, she reaches the first door and her fist freezes in mid-air as she goes to knock. The door is wide open. Her heart starts beating faster and her breath catches in her throat as she looks down at the bloodstains beneath her feet. She looks back down the corridor to the stairwell door and curses herself for not noticing the red, smeared footprints on the light-coloured carpet. Deep red, dried blood smears are all over the high gloss white wooden stairwell door. She slowly follows the bloody footprints on the carpet and looks towards the end of the corridor. Her heart skips a beat as she sees the man that is facing her. He has drool coming from his mouth and his eyes are all bloodshot, like he has a serious disease. His skin is drawn and tight against his face, and Sarah can see that his normally dark black skin has gone shades paler, almost grey.

The man rocks gently as he stares at her and his head rolls about, seemingly uncontrolled. He is dressed in white shorts and a once-white vest top that is now heavily stained from blood and saliva.

The man groans and starts to shuffle slowly towards her; his movements are slow and jerky as he moves. He slowly spasms and twitches, flicks his arms out, and causes his head to jerk quickly to one side.

Terrified, Sarah stands still, watching the man shuffling towards her. Then she comes to and darts forward into the open doorway with a squeal, slamming the door behind her and running into the lounge area.

The apartment has the same layout as hers, but with different furniture and décor, which makes it feel surreal. She pulls the knife from her pocket and turns back to face the door, listening intently, her heartbeat thudding in her ears.

An old zombie woman shuffles on thick carpet slippers into the lounge. Saliva dribbles from her old and puckered mouth and coats the front of her nightgown. She inches towards Sarah, the bloodshot eyes staring at the tender skin of Sarah's bare neck.

Sarah's heart is pounding and the blood rushes through her temples, deafening her senses. She waits for the sound of the man against the door and tightens the grip on the knife handle, but a sudden noise behind her causes her to spin around. She screams as she sees the old woman, a massive, ragged gash in her neck. She lunges at Sarah with her lips pulled back.

Sarah yells and jumps backwards, at the same time thrusting the knife forward, plunging the sharp blade directly into the old woman's chest. The zombie is knocked back, but then continues forward again. Sarah backs away, staring at the knife handle embedded in the woman's chest.

She is trapped in the short corridor between the lounge and the front door and, within a couple of steps, her back is pressing against the door.

The old woman keeps coming, each small shuffling step bringing her closer and closer to Sarah, who stares in horror at the skin that is torn away from the open neck wound.

Sarah waits until the old woman is two or three steps away and lunges forward again, grabbing the knife handle and pulling it free. She stabs, plunging the knife back into the zombie woman's chest, but again gets no reaction.

The dead woman is pushing against Sarah and has again pulled her lips back to reveal worn-down old, yellowing teeth.

Sarah stabs furiously in a blind panic, and then uses her hands to drive the woman away.

The old woman zombie falls to the floor from the power of the blows, and Sarah yanks the blade free and staggers back to the door. The elderly zombie slowly sits up and starts bending forward to stand.

'Oh ... fuck off,' Sarah cries out and, without thinking, pushes the door handle down and pulls the door open.

The zombie man is standing in front of her, and Sarah screams again and lashes out with the knife, slashing him across the face. His skin peels apart like dried fruit and blood seeps down into his mouth, turning the saliva pink.

Sarah feels the old woman against the back of her leg and spins around to see the woman reaching towards her. She stamps down on the zombie woman's head and drives her face hard into the floor, feeling the crunch as the nose is broken and teeth are knocked out.

The zombie man staggers in, spitting bloody drool, and Sarah stabs out hard and fast, puckering his chest and abdomen. She moves backwards, but gets stuck by the old woman's body.

In desperation, she raises the knife high in both hands and drives it into the skull of the zombie man as he lunges forward for the bite. The blade forces through the skull into the brain, and the force of the blow drives the zombie down onto the floor. Whimpering and full of panic, Sarah jumps over his body and dashes out into the corridor. She screams loudly as she sees another zombie coming out of the next apartment, shuffling towards her. Sarah backs away down the corridor, unarmed, the knife still embedded in the zombie man's head. She backs down to the stairwell door and turns to run away, suddenly seeing another ravaged and bloodied face staring at her through the glass pane from the stairwell.

'FUCKING HELL!' Sarah moves away from the door.

Turning round, she sees the old woman zombie crawling out of the apartment doorway into the corridor. The other zombie man advances slowly and Sarah hears the door being pushed open, behind her.

With a yell, she slams her body into the door, sending the zombie behind it flying backwards. She spins around, trapped again, desperately trying to think of a way out. She looks down at the wall and the bright red plastic case of the fire hose and instantly starts tugging at the large door to open it up.

The door stays shut and Sarah loses valuable seconds fumbling to open the clasp.

The stairwell door starts to open and Sarah kicks out hard, slamming the plate glass into the face of the zombie. Blood spurts out from his broken nose, coating the glass pane. Sarah pulls at the hose and the heavy metal head, yanking it free of the reel; the large red, metal head has arrows depicting ON and OFF.

Sarah fumbles with the tap head and twists it the wrong way, in her panic. The door swings open and the zombie lunges into the corridor. Sarah swings the heavy metal hose-head and batters him across the face, forcing him to spin into the wall behind him. She twists at the tap head and hears as water surges through the hose, sending it rigid – but no water comes out. She pulls the lever and gets thrown backwards onto the floor by the sudden release of the water shooting out of the end. The hose dances and bangs against the walls, forcing gallons of water out into the corridor, soaking everything. Sarah is drenched within seconds, and has to fight against the powerful spray to take hold of the metal head. She picks it up and turns it back towards the stairwell door, straight at the zombie man. The powerful jet of water knocks him back through the door and into the stairwell. The door swings closed, causing the water to spray back and soak Sarah again. She spins round on her backside and directs the jet at the next zombie man, again hitting him from close range at centre mass and knocking him clean off his feet and down onto the floor. The old zombie woman has crawled close to her victim, and Sarah forces the jet of water directly into her face. The woman's skin is pummelled and forced back as she gargles and chokes on the water, but she keeps crawling forward; Sarah leans over with the hose so that it is right in front of her and the jets force the zombie woman's head back – as the water is pumped down her throat.

Finally, the old woman dies again as her lungs fill with water and her stomach lining expands from the sudden fluid intake. Sarah gets to her feet and switches the lever off; the sudden loss of pressure causing the hose to drop down a few inches as she turns back to the stairwell door.

Sarah marches forward and kicks the door open to see the zombie man just getting to his feet, balancing on the edge of the top step.

'Fuck you,' Sarah shouts and pulls the lever back.

The powerful surge of water takes the zombie clean off his feet and down onto the next level. Sarah pulls the hose through and slowly steps down the stairs, her feet squelching in the sodden carpet. Sarah directs the hose at the zombie, spraying it across the short landing and down the next flight of stairs, a look of grim determination on her face. The hose extends far enough for Sarah to jet the zombie out of the next door and into the corridor of the 20th floor; then she rushes forward, spraying it further down the corridor, buying herself time to run back to her own apartment, tears streaming down her already-soaked face.

Sarah sprints to her door, lurching through and slamming it behind her. Then she slumps down, sobbing and soaked through. Her mind races at what she has witnessed. When this first happened she'd suspected it was a mass breakdown of civil order and general violence that had happened recently in London and other English cities. Then she spoke to her father who said it was everywhere. Sarah has been running his words through her mind ever since. What did he mean by *everywhere*?

He couldn't mean worldwide – surely not the whole world? Zombies and vampires are make-believe, something invented for the movies. They can't exist; something so frequently seen on television can't just happen ... but all the things I have seen must be believed. Zombies have risen up and are roaming the land. Sarah sobs for a long time, unleashing the pent-up misery and isolation of the last few days; crying hard for her family, friends and the people she had seen being taken down. Tears course down her cheeks and her body heaves as the sadness pours out of her. Eventually, wet through and shivering from shock, she staggers to the bathroom and pulls off her soaking clothes. She uses the thick, cotton towel to dry her body, moving like a robot, without expression – thinking only of what she'd just witnessed a few floors above her – thinking of the decaying bodies that stank of death with greying skin and saliva drooling out of their mouths, the red blood-shot eyes and the horrific injuries on them. She had stabbed that woman again and again but still she kept coming, and Sarah replays the action in her head, feeling as the knife bit into the rib bones and jarred her wrist, the suction of the skin as she pulled the knife out, and the fresh blood spurting from the injuries she had caused.

The thoughts and images become too much and her stomach heaves as she drops down with her head in the toilet bowl, puking up the tiny tuna meal she had forced down. She stays there for a long time, retching and sobbing into the toilet.

Chapter 6

We sit in the Saxon with the engine switched off. We only left Salisbury a short time ago, and we have already passed through several small villages as we progress through the country roads. The first village centre only had a handful of undead in the centre, all of them gathered once again in the heart of the village, shuffling and groaning in the scorching sun.

'They're not getting much of a tan, are they? Considering how long they've been out in this heat,' I say to Dave, who is sitting next to me, staring at the mini-horde as we drive past.

'No, Mr. Howie,' he replies.

'You'd think they'd be burnt to buggery by now.'

'Possibly.'

'But then, there's something in the body isn't there, that causes the skin to get tanned? I guess dead people just don't tan very well.'

'Pigs do.'

'What?'

'Pigs can get sunburnt.'

'No way ... pigs can't get a suntan.'

'They can.'

'Well … I always thought that cows explode, if they don't get milked.'

'Do they?'

'I don't know – I heard that they did.'

'Oh … I've never seen one explode on its own.'

'Well … maybe it's not true then … hang on … what do you mean … not on its own.'

'Well, I haven't.'

'So, have you seen a cow explode, then?'

'Yes.'

'How did it explode?'

'I blew it up.'

'You blew a cow up?'

'Yes.'

'Why? How did you blow a cow up?'

'I put explosives on it and blew it up.'

'You did what?! You can't go around blowing cows up.'

'I had to.'

'Why? Why on earth did you have to blow the poor cow up?'

'To kill the cow herder.'

'What? You blew a fucking cow up, just to kill a cow herder?'

'Yes.'

'That makes no sense, why didn't you just kill *him*.'

'I did.'

'No … I mean, why didn't you kill him some other way, like shooting or stabbing or strangulation or something other than blowing him up.'

'It had to look like an accident.'

'A fucking accident …Oh, yeah … 'cause cows are always exploding where I live … how on earth can you make an exploding cow look like an accident?'

'He was a courier for explosives.'

'Oh, I see. Well … I guess that makes sense then … I think?'

'He carried explosives for the insurgents, so we rigged the cow to blow up and took him out.'

'Oh, where was that then?'

The Undead Day Five

'I can't say, Mr. Howie.'

I knew he was going to say that.

'Fuck me, look at that lot …' I shout and hear the recruits scrambling forward to try and peer out the front.

'Zombies ahead,' Tucker shouts from his look-out position on the GPMG.

'No shit … really, Tucker … where are they?' Cookey yells back.

'Ahead,' Tucker shouts down.

'I was being sarcastic,' Cookey calls out.

'What?' Tucker yells.

'I SAID I WAS BEING SARCASTIC,' Cookey bellows out.

'You want some elastic? Try my bag, there might be some in there, mate.'

'Oh, for fucks sake,' Cookey groans.

'Give up mate, it's a lost cause,' McKinney offers.

So here we are, sitting in the Saxon, looking at a massed horde blocking the road ahead of us. The village doesn't look that big, with just one main road going through a collection of shops and houses. There is a village green off to the right, bordered by a metal fence, and the horde is gathered up against the fence. They start slowly turning around to face us.

'Well, that's a shitload of zombies,' I say to Dave.

'It is, Mr. Howie.'

'Do you think that the A … P … C … will get through them?'

'Might do, Mr. Howie,'

'Right lads, buckle up,' I call back.

'TUCKER, HANG ON TIGHT,' I yell up.

'What?' he yells back.

'Ah, he'll be all right.' I restart the engine and push my foot down, making the engine scream with power.

I slowly lift the clutch and the vehicle shoots forward and … stalls.

'Not a word …' I say, as I hear sniggers coming from behind me and try again, going a bit easier with the clutch this time. The vehicle surges forward, gathering speed quite quickly. We plough into the front of the horde and the hard metal square front detonates their heads and bodies, sending them spinning off and knocking more over.

I plough through and feel a slight bump as the massive tyres crush the undead beneath us. The vehicle hardly rocks on the suspension and, within seconds, we are through them, leaving a trail of broken and squashed bodies behind us. The lads all cheer and whistle and I can hear Tucker shouting something. I stop the Saxon and look over at Dave.

'Did you see that? Fucking brilliant, this thing is awesome.' I sound like an excited child, babbling away. 'They were smashed apart and we hardly felt a thing.'

'Yes.'

I use the side wing mirrors to look back, and see the mangled remains and those not so injured picking themselves up off the ground.

'Would be a shame to just leave them there, mate,' I say to Dave with a grin.

'Do you want to go back again?' he asks me.

'Yeah, we could – or we could do it the old-fashioned way.'

Dave turns to look back at the recruits in the back.

'Blowers, get those bayonets from the box and show the rest how to fit them on.'

'Yes, DAVE,' Blowers answers promptly and somehow makes the word 'Dave' sound like 'Sarge'. I reach down to the floor and lift my axe up; it is all shiny and clean, feeling nice and heavy. I test the blade with my thumb and jerk my hand back from the unexpected sharpness.

'I sharpened it,' Dave says.

'Bloody hell, thanks, mate. You still got the knives then,' I say, as he suddenly has them in his hands; I didn't even see where they came from.

'I put new blades on these too,' he says, staring along the sharp edges.

I can hear the recruits talking quietly, and then clicking noises; one of them yelps.

'I fucking told you it was sharp, didn't I,' Blowers says with

The Undead Day Five

scorn. Then, after a few minutes, he shouts out that they are all ready. I feel the adrenalin start pumping and the anger is knocking at the door, waiting to be let out. I pull the axe and climb down from the high driver's position. The zombies are shuffling closer to us and I hold the axe down at my side as I walk around the front of the vehicle to meet Dave as he climbs out.

The lads jump down and walk back towards us, holding their rifles carefully due to the massive, nasty-looking blades at the end.

'Safeties on,' Dave says to them, and they all look down to check the side of their weapons.

'Strike and move, use the weight of the weapon to drive them back with repeated stabs to the chest and torso. Use the butt of the weapon for blunt trauma. The bayonets are sharp and will slice through their jugulars easily. Be very careful if you have to fire the weapon in close confines, the round will rip through the body and come out the other side,' instructs Dave – an impressively long speech from him.

Finally Dave turns to me and nods. I start to walk towards the encroaching zombies and stop.

'Ready lads?' I ask of the young recruits.

'Yes, Mr. Howie,' they nearly all mutter. I turn and stalk towards the undead. The last few metres I stare hard at the nearest one, a large-built male, and I feel my eyelids twitching, my mind filling with the image of my beloved parents being bitten by one of these foul things. The axe is down at my side as I step closer. Time slows and I feel my right fist clenching and, before I have any idea what I'm doing, I have slammed my hard fist into the side of the zombie's head. I follow through with the punch and slam him across the road. He staggers into another undead but stays on his feet, and I'm on him before he can react, punching again and again with my right fist. The blows send him down onto the ground and I go still. Waiting. Breathing. I feel them surround me, I feel their presence, and I close my eyes in anticipation.

The danger of being so close to these evil things thrills me. The infection they carry is all around me, their teeth are being pulled back and they step and shuffle closer and closer. *But I am death. And I come for you.* I open my eyes and scream into the air as I spin the axe up and around, slicing through skin and bone. I drive the cutting edge towards necks and feel the sharpened blade bite and slice through their evil, tainted, infected skin.

I step backwards and drive down a massive, overhead strike, cleaving through a skull and watching as brains burst out and the head implodes. My senses are heightened and I feel one lunging at my back. I step back and drive my elbow into his face, dropping him instantly. The axe is alive, an extension of my body. We are one, and we destroy those that stand before us. I chop into heads and necks, slicing faces off, biting the vicious blade into collarbones and spinal columns as they fall at my feet. I plough forward, swinging and killing. A quick glance over and I see Dave moving like water through them, his arms spinning with grace and beauty. A strange man with an amazing gift – moving like a ballet dancer – his whole body poised, flexing, bending and stretching with each killing blow. He darts forward and plunges the knives into the chest of a zombie woman, his arms a blur as he rapidly stabs and then slices through the jugular and drops down to avoid the spray that soaks into the eyes of the next zombie, blinding him. Dave spins around the back, dragging the blade after him as he lunges forward, driving the point of his other knife into the throat of the next one. I go back to work and cleave my way through the bastard horde, the evil foul things that walk this world after their natural life has expired. I kill and maim and leave broken, undead bodies behind me. Then I break through into a clearing and rejoice as I see a fresh and densely-packed group ahead of me. The anger has only just warmed up, it has stretched out and flexed muscles and is now ready for the proper workout. I look back and see Blowers driving into them with a look of pure fury on his face, Cookey by his side, the banter and easy jokes gone now as they tear the undead apart. Tucker is screaming with hatred and fear, hacking away. McKinney, Smith, and all of them are in amongst them, and the bodies fall down with hacked and bloodied injuries. I turn back to the horde ahead of me just as Dave gets to my side. We stare at each other, words not needed, and we charge together, roaring into battle. Dave launches himself high

The Undead Day Five

into the air and comes down into them, his knives doing the deadly business of sending them back to the hell from whence they came. My axe is breaking them apart.

I pick my targets one by one.

A neck gets cleaved and the head drops down. I swing the blunt end back and I crush a skull. I drop the axe low and strike up into bollocks, destroying the undead's chances of ever breeding his evil spawn. I spin and swing the axe behind me, chopping a zombie arm off at the shoulder. Then I go low again and take a leg off at the knee joint. This doesn't kill them, but it pleases me to maim and hurt and make them fall down onto the bloody and slick ground. We keep going: chopping, slicing, hacking, and destroying – until one dirty zombie remains and we gather round him.

Silent faces.

Hard breathing.

The zombie turns around and around, unable to decide which one of us to try and bite.

Me, Blowers, Cookey, McKinney, Smith, Tucker, Graves, Reese, Hewitt, and Dave stand around this one remaining filthy, dirty, evil, zombie fucker.

We stare hard at him and I see the anger inside each of them. There is glory here, glory in battling alongside brave warriors such as these. Dave steps forward and takes the zombie by the back of his hair, wrenching his head back and pulling him off his feet. I roar and raise the axe high, driving it down into the exposed neck. As the blow lands, the recruits pile in and the zombie is punctured by eight sharp points from eight sharp bayonets being pushed by eight brave young warriors that have been pushed to the brink by these evil things. The body is hacked apart, unrecognisable within minutes. We walk silently back to the Saxon, taking long gulps of water from our canteens and nodding at each other.

'That was fucking beautiful,' Cookey says quietly, to nods and murmurs of agreement from all around him. We use wipes to clean the blood from our weapons and skin and then load back into the Saxon.

'At least you didn't bum them this time, Cookey,' Blowers says.

'Fuck you, Blowers – you were stabbing them in the willy,' Cookey retorts.

'The willy? Are you ten or something?' McKinney joins in.

'You were stabbing them in their zombie willies.' Tucker laughs loudly at the infantile language being used.

'You can all get fucked!' Cookey shouts, and the abuse goes on. I drive the Saxon away from the village, away from the devastation and the bodies lying festering in the sun.

Chapter 7

All over the world, the infection feels the losses from these survivors. The infection feels its size dwindling as the fighters become more deadly and more cunning in their resistance. Small groups gather and organise themselves, securing supplies and learning how to take the deadly hosts down during the daytime, and then hiding themselves away in strong and secure locations that the zombies cannot penetrate.

They take away ladders and ropes, lock strong doors and remove the keys, use the underground networks and anything they find that still works. The rats have progressed the rate of infection significantly, and their small, wiry bodies have been able to get into places that the human hosts were unable to access, but they are easy to kill and put down. Through millions of eyes, the infection watches these fighters and it understands that in order to survive it must target these first.

The infection again watches as the one called Howie leads his fighters in an attack and kills many hosts, and the infection watches through those millions of eyes to see when they will reappear so it can send the rats into them. Inside the minds of the test hosts, the infection continues to play with the brain and learn more of the complex secrets this thing possesses. It already understands that the hosts were not fully in control of these brains, and, like itself, it knows the brain is a work in progress, still in the early stages of evolution. The infection allows the mind to access memories and knowledge, but the billions and billions of *images and thought processes just cause confusion as they are in no order and have no sense. But the infection controls many now and can work on these images while the hosts rest and repair. The infection now knows that the same strengths, cunning, and guile possessed by the fighters are locked inside these minds, and it will work hard and fast to unlock them. Unlock them, not just to take more hosts, but to fight back.*

To buy itself time, the infection urges the rats on, devouring everything in their path. The success of the rats has spread across the world, and soon they are scurrying over every street and road worldwide. **Bite, but don't kill** *is the message constantly replayed in their tiny brains. They work as a super-organism, and even the hardest and toughest resisters are consumed with panic as the black plague comes for them.*

Chapter 8

We enter another small village and find a horde gathered outside a florist's. The once beautiful flowers in the window are now wilting.

This horde is small in number, compared to the previous one, maybe a dozen of them at most; I see a child zombie in the group this time. Thankfully, I haven't killed any child zombies ... yet. A couple of days ago I would have blanched at the thought of it and been sickened to the core. But now I've hardened and they are not children any more. They are undead, and they will kill given the chance. They must be dealt with, like any other undead.

'Can we stop please, Mr. Howie,' Dave says to me, snapping me out of my thoughts.

'Yes, mate. Why? What's up?' I ask him as I bring the huge Saxon to a halt, causing the recruits to cram forward.

'Practise,' Dave says simply and indicates the small horde.

'Okay, mate.'

The recruits clamber out and gather around Dave at the back of the vehicle. I look at the horde, itching to go for them and take them all out.

'You did well with the last lot, but you were clumsy and slow. We are going to practise on these,' Dave informs the recruits as I lean on my axe.

'Take off the bayonets and I will show you some basic techniques for using it as a bladed weapon.' The recruits do as instructed and remove the bayonets from the end of the assault rifles.

'Now ... weapons back in the Saxon and follow me.'

They place their assault rifles back in the Saxon and then walk with him towards the horde.

The sun feels uncomfortably hot.

The zombies have turned towards us and started their slow shuffle, but I parked well back to give us time to arrange ourselves – so there is no immediate rush. The recruits gather around Dave, holding the knives self-consciously out in front of themselves, glancing at each other and at the horde.

'Now you can stab them in the chest, but that won't kill them – it buys you time and the weight of the thrust can drive them backwards – but it is not a killing blow. Do you understand?' Dave asks and looks at them in turn as they nod.

'The only sure way that I have found of killing them is the neck and head. Even after repeated stabs to the chest and abdomen they still fight back, so they don't die like normal people – but they do bleed. The bleeding is different though, a few stabs that would normally render a man lifeless within seconds do not seem to affect them in the same way. The way 'round that is to cause them a massive loss of blood that even they cannot cope with. Now watch.' Dave walks towards the horde, holding his knives down at his sides; the nearest undead is an adult male, middle-aged and fat. He is wearing a pink, frilly dressing gown that is open; his wobbly bits dangle as he shuffles along.

'Now take it easy, Cookey – I know what you are looking at,' Blowers mutters to a few sniggers.

'Yeah, you're just jealous 'cos he's bigger than you,' Cookey retorts. Dave turns back to look hard at the lads, who fall silent under his intense gaze. Then he simply walks up to the zombie and stabs him once in the chest and leaves the knife embedded in. He quickly steps back as the zombie bares his teeth and lunges forward.

'See here, this one is now stabbed through the chest with a long-bladed weapon. This would normally drop even the strongest of men, but he does not even flinch,' Dave calls out, and the recruits watch with interest as the undead continues to shuffle forward with the knife handle sticking out of his chest. Dave steps in and stabs with the other knife, driving that one down into his lungs.

'So now, he has two knives in his chest. I have punctured one of his lungs, but still he does not react, nor does he slow down,' Dave points at the undead.

He then steps forward and quickly pulls both blades out, causing the zombie to stagger forward a little from the pressure of the pull.

'Now, a lot of the damage from stabbing is done when the weapon is removed. The embedded blade can cause a seal around arteries and capillaries, and the removal of the weapon breaks that seal, but here we see that although there is blood loss from the wounds, it is far more reduced than with a normal person. Their blood congeals much faster than ours, which means that they can withstand injuries such as this.' Dave turns back to the recruits to make sure they understand. Most of them nod and murmur with interest.

'So, a stab will only be of use if it has a single purpose to drive them back, like this,' Dave lunges with frightening speed and stabs repeatedly into the chest and abdomen of the zombie. His arms blur, and although I have seen him move in several battles now, I am still amazed. The zombie is forced backwards from the many punctures and eventually falls down onto the ground. Dave steps away and faces the recruits, not in the slightest out of breath.

'He is still alive, or dead … undead.' Dave scratches his head and stares down at the zombie trying to rise back up.

'Anyway, the repeated wounds have not killed him, so we have to look to the rapid blood loss.' Dave steps forward and sweeps his blade across the zombie's throat, stepping behind him and facing back to the recruits.

'See the arterial blood spraying out? There is nothing known that can congeal, stop, or replenish that amount of blood loss in that short space of time.'

The recruits watch the bright red jet of blood spurting out in waves from the throat, soaking the pink dressing gown and the ground beneath. Within seconds, the zombie rolls over and is still.

'So, we go for the throat or the brain, but the brain is protected by the hard casing of the skull and requires a significant use of force.' Dave steps to the next zombie and lightly taps the point of his knife into the skull.

'The skull has to be thick to prevent injury to the brain, so here I am hitting the skull with light force, and other than causing minor puncture wounds, I do not affect the brain at all. Now ... as I increase the force used, you will see that even a significant amount does not penetrate the bone.' Dave keeps walking round the adult female zombie, digging the tip of the knife into her head.

'Now, in order to penetrate and drive into the brain, you must apply direct force, do not sweep or slash. Drive the point of the weapon directly into the top of the head.' Dave pulls his arm and slams it down, causing the knife to dig into the skull. Then Dave lets go and the body falls to the ground, with the knife still stuck in the head.

'Blood is slippery and can easily cause you to lose grip on the handle, and you need a similar amount of force to pull the knife back out. You can see that with a wet handle and the weight of the body dropping, you could lose your grip and then have no weapon.' Dave bends over and grabs the fallen zombie female by the ankle, dragging her over to the recruits.

'I want each of you to feel how hard that blade is stuck in.' The lads all gather around the female zombie's head and take it in turns to pull at the handle, remarking to each other, in serious tones, how really hard it is stuck in there. This has got to be one of the most surreal scenes I have ever witnessed. A group of eighteen-year-old lads standing round a dead zombie, discussing how well the knife is stuck in her brain, in a quiet village in southern England.

Dave then puts a foot on the zombie's shoulder and pulls the knife out, then leans down and wipes the blood on the back of her nightdress.

'Right, I want each of you to find a zombie and try it out,' Dave says, as he cleans the blade.

Blowers, Cookey, McKinney, and Smith all move forward to do as Dave says. Tucker hesitates, then he too moves into the crowd. I watch the lads dodge around and through the zombie horde and try to avoid their last-second lunges. Blowers and Cookey both go for the same zombie and start arguing about whose it is, until Tucker grabs the back of the head and slices cleanly through the neck, dropping the body before smiling and walking back to Dave. They both stare after him, open-mouthed.

A determined look crosses Cookey's face and he stalks off to viciously pull a head back hard and gouges down into the flesh, sawing away until he almost decapitates it from the body. Eventually, they are all dead, apart from the zombie child who drools and starts toward Dave. The rest all watch with mixed looks of horror and revulsion. Dave stares hard at the zombie and starts forward with his knives. Before he has taken two steps I have rushed in with the axe and sliced clean through the neck; the body falls slowly to the floor, blood pumping out onto the hot tarmac. I stare back at the recruits until they all look down to their feet or off into the distance.

'It's not a child any more – they are not people. They will kill you and turn you into one of them. Don't hesitate next time.' I walk back to the vehicle with a mixture of feelings: guilty because it was still a child's body and everything we are ever taught in life is to protect children at all costs; they are the future. Even though I told them it wasn't a child, it has left me feeling numb.

The fuel gauge drops steadily and I realise the biggest flaw of having a vehicle this size is that the fuel consumption is so high. We will need to re-fuel before too long. Dave looks at me, having followed my gaze. I can see that he remembers the last time we tried to refuel by putting diesel into a petrol-only tank. We almost got caught by a massive horde as night fell.

'Don't worry, mate, I'll make sure it's the right kind this time.'

'Thanks, Mr. Howie.'

Before long, we pass through yet another village, but this one is devoid of life. I slow down so we can look closely, but there are no bloodstains or broken windows. Nothing. This doesn't feel right; every village we have passed through has had some zombies in it.

'Who is on look-out?' I call back to the recruits.

'McKinney,' Reese shouts back, as he is the closest to my end.

'Ask him if he can see anything from up there.'

Reese stands up and speaks with McKinney, who yells down.

'He said no, sir. He can't see anyone.'

'Strange,' I say, and Reese continues leaning forward to look out of the front window.

'Certainly is quiet,' he murmurs.

'What's up?' one of them calls from the back.

'We're going through another village, but it is completely dead, if you'll pardon the expression. There's no one here,' Reese calls back to them.

I hear more of the lads shuffling along to try and glimpse out of the front windows.

'Can I open the rear doors to look out?' one of them shouts. It sounds like Blowers, but he must be at the back and the vehicle is loud.

'Good idea,' I shout out, and the message gets relayed.

I suddenly hear more noise from the massive wheels going on the road. We drive out of the village and into a country lane. There are wooden signposts stuck into the verge advertising a Farmer's Fete this weekend. Then, as the road bends around, I see the top of a large white marquee in a big field off to the left. As we get closer, I can see the tops of cars and vans parked in the adjacent field and a gap in the hedge connecting the two fields. The signposts indicate to turn left for parking. I slow down to try and get a better view, but the hedgerow is too high. I hear McKinney shouting and I decrease the speed even more, waiting for the message to be relayed.

'McKinney says they are all in the field by the tent, loads of 'em, sir,' Reese leans forward and tells me.

'Well, we've got to have a look, really,' I say to Dave as I stop the Saxon.

The Undead Day Five

'There are bloody loads in there, sir,' McKinney says as I clamber up onto the roof. I stand up and look over the hedge and see a large, flat field with a big white marquee off to one side. There is a roped-off circular central area and then some smaller tents and marquees around the outside. This explains where all of the village zombies have gone – they are all here. Hundreds of them have gathered in and around the large marquee – hundreds of undead in various types of nightclothes or completely naked. From a distance it looks like some weird sex party or a fancy dress shindig, with everyone coming in their pyjamas.

'Fucking look at that,' I mutter to myself. 'You don't see that every day, now do you?'

'No, sir,' McKinney answers.

'Well, we can't stop and kill every zombie we see – but I feel bad if we just leave them here for some poor helpless soul to wander into,' I say to McKinney.

'Do you want me to use this, sir?' I look at McKinney and he taps the top of the GPMG.

'Dave, how much ammo do we have for the GPMG,' I shout down and then see Dave is already climbing up onto the roof.

'Oh, sorry mate, I didn't mean to yell.'

'That's okay, Mr. Howie – we've got loads,' Dave says.

'All yours then, McKinney,' I say to him and move off to the side so I am well out of the way.

A large grin forms on his face and McKinney yanks back the lever and aims the gun into the middle of the horde. He hesitates for a few seconds, and glances at me again.

'Mate, you don't have to do it, someone else will ...' I say to him.

He shrugs and lets rip with the heavy machine gun.

The noise invades the quiet air and the zombies immediately start falling as they are torn apart by the heavy calibre weapon. The recruits all look up at McKinney and I know some of them will be jealous that he has the chance to use it and kill so many. Movement catches my eye and I see Dave waving at me, pointing to the GPMG. I shout out for McKinney to stop firing. Once silent, I shake my head from the sudden cessation of noise and look down at Dave. He has got a large metal container out from the back of the Saxon and opens the lid. The things inside are instantly recognisable; I've seen them a thousand times on movies, but never in real life.

Hand grenades. Dave gathers the recruits around him, apart from McKinney, and shows them how to remove the pin and keep hold of the lever, then pull the arm back for a long throw. Dave leads them all up the lane and into the car park, then through the gap in the hedge until they are in the field and staring at the already reduced numbers of the zombies.

I can see Dave talking to them, but cannot hear what he is saying – from his movement I guess that he is telling them to throw it far and then find cover.

There is a large tractor with an evil-looking, giant metal contraption fitted to the end. Dave leads them all over so that the tractor attachment is between them and the zombies. He then pulls the pin out of his grenade and uses a big overhead sweep of his arm to launch the grenade into the middle of the packed crowd, shouting 'GRENADE' as he does so.

The explosion that takes place a few seconds later is a lot bigger than I'd expected, and I see several bodies blown up a few feet into the air and many more drop down from the shrapnel ripping through legs and stomachs. Dave then makes them all take turns to throw a grenade each and shout 'GRENADE' as they launch it.

McKinney and I watch with '… ooh's' and '… aaah's' like a fireworks' display – as the grenades explode and cause devastation to the horde. The zombies closest to the exploding grenades are obliterated with each loud percussive bang. The lads finish lobbing their grenades and I can see that they are smiling and laughing at the carnage that has been caused.

Dave gives me a thumbs up as they leave the field and it's safe for McKinney to continue. The GPMG starts up again and, within seconds, they are all dead – or at least down and unable to get back up from their awful injuries.

'That was fucking amazing, did you see them explode? I fucking love blowing stuff up,' Darren Smith says excitedly as they walk back to the Saxon and load up into the rear.

'Are we going to stop at every village on the way, sir?' Blowers shouts to me.

'It would be nice, but we don't have the time, mate,' I reply, thinking how everyone is calling me Sir or Mr. Howie now. I'm just a shift manager for a supermarket, how the hell did I end up leading a squadron of zombie killers across the country?

Chapter 9

The infection recognises this group of resisters that keep cutting it down. It watches the one they call Howie who is standing further away, watching as the hosts are destroyed and the infection is once again diminished.

The infection now controls billions of hosts across the world, so this handful of losses does not impact it greatly, but the infection feels the loss. Although it does not have emotions or feelings, it has an understanding that this must be stopped. The resistance fighters grow stronger and their numbers increase, as they join together and wreak devastation during the daytime. They use bigger and better tools to aid their killing, and find new ways to destroy the hosts. The infection knows, from the chemicals inside the hosts, that it should be feeling anger, and it begins to understand what revenge means. It continues to experiment on the few host bodies across the world that it keeps isolated to practise with. Those few hosts, separated from the hordes, suffer incredible amounts of torture as the infection floods them with the chemicals it learns to produce. The hosts scream in pain and collapse on the floor with rigid tension when the pain becomes too much. They dance and jump around and move quicker and quicker as the infection learns to control the flow of electrical impulses to the tendons, nerves, and muscles.

They break down and cry when they are filled with a sudden overwhelming sense of sadness and loss, weeping uncontrollably and pounding their fists into their heads in desperation. Then they suddenly burst up and start giggling with glee; the giggles become louder until they are laughing uncontrollably with the sudden switch in chemicals coursing through their bodies. The chemical flow is switched again and the laughing stops; they become suddenly serious and stare hard into the distance as the infection pumps the blood and makes them feel anger – then the anger increases until they are filled with a burning rage – a rage that needs to be fed with violence and an urge to destroy everything around it. The infection feels this rage through the hosts' bodies and knows this is something it can use. The practise hosts are pumped full of this deadly hormone and they are released from control to do as they wish, and they move with lightning speed to pound and destroy anything near them. Those that are alone, without access to inanimate objects, turn on themselves as the blind fury possesses them – they gouge their skin and bite their fingers off, then pummel their own bodies with vicious blows, breaking ribs and knee joints. Some of the control hosts are near other host bodies and they turn on them with an amazing ferocity. They attack and kill the other hosts with an incredible strength and the infection allows them to continue, watching through many eyes: the attackers, the witnesses, and the victims.

The rage is too strong, though, and the control hosts spend too long on one body, ripping it apart with their bare hands and teeth, shredding the flesh and pulling the insides out to throw them down on the ground so they can be stamped upon. The control hosts hurt themselves to the point that they cannot function and drop down to the floor – being so unable to cause the destruction they crave, they turn on themselves and rip their own bodies apart. The infection has found something here, something it can use, but it has to learn to harness this power. So, as the first control hosts are killed by their own demented actions, the infection takes more control hosts and, in every land, there are single zombies that suddenly stop rolling their heads and groaning. They look forward and intelligence comes back into their eyes – as they step away from the hordes they are with, to stand alone.

Chapter 10

Sarah wakes on the sofa; the sobbing and crying had left her feeling drained and she slept fitfully for a few hours, with horrific images coursing through her sleeping mind. What she experienced has shocked her to the core, and a deep feeling of sadness, loss, and desperation overwhelm her. She doesn't know how long she can keep going, unable to leave her apartment and struggling to survive on just the few tins of food she has left. She paces through her apartment, which helps her to think and forces her mind to work rationally. She can now use work skills to break the problems down into small chunks.

'What do we know?' She starts speaking to herself as she would at work when faced with a difficult or complex matter.

'I'm on the 14th floor and I only saw them on the 21st floor. There were no signs of them on any floors between here and the 21st floor. Now … there is one on the 20th floor. He did not see which floor I ran to, so, unless he can smell me, he cannot find me and I was soaked with water – which will remove any smells. But then I did leave a water trail behind me. Okay … so he *could* find me. But there were no signs of them on the other floors. I have only

The Undead Day Five

a few tins of food left, but plenty of water – so I can survive – but it will get very hard. Priorities ... I need more food. If they are dead zombies then they cannot survive forever without food or water – they have been outside in the street now for days and I haven't seen them eat or drink anything. So, I need to eat and wait for them to die, or die again, or just fuck off and leave me alone. But, in order for me to survive, I need food and that means going back out there for more supplies.' She stands still, as she realises what must be done. She nods to herself with quiet resolution.

'I have to get more food. Going up is no good, so this time I will go down. I also need weapons.' She rushes into the small kitchen and goes through her cutlery drawers. Waving knives and rolling pins about, she practises with each item, but the knives are no good; stabbing at them seems ineffective. She moves from room to room, looking for anything that could be used. Eventually, back in the kitchen, she finds a large, wooden broomstick that had been left by the previous tenants. She always thought it was odd to have a wooden broom in a tiny, carpeted apartment. Sarah takes the broom and holds it up; it isn't heavy, but it is long. She rummages through more drawers and pulls out a roll of brown parcel tape that she used to secure her moving-in boxes. She takes a long-bladed kitchen knife and tapes it securely to the end of the broomstick handle; she then moves into the lounge and practises lunging and stabbing with it. It isn't perfect, but it will have to do, and she knows that she has to leave now and try again or the fear will become too much and she will never be able to leave.

She walks to the door and extends her hand, grasping the handle and pausing to calm her breathing and her rapidly beating heart. She then yanks the door open and jumps out into the corridor, like an Amazonian warrior – holding the broomstick out in front, like a spear. She faces one way and jumps around to face the other side of the empty corridor. She gets to the stairwell and each step brings more fear, but courage grows after each step is taken.

Sarah peers through the glass pane. There is nothing but silence all around; the only signs of her prior encounter are the wet stains on the carpet, but even they are drying quickly in the hot air. Sarah breathes deeply and starts down the stairs, taking each step slowly to make sure her footsteps are masked from noise by the soft carpet. She reaches the door to the 13th floor and again looks through the window into another empty corridor. She advances slowly and, this time, she opens the fire hose cabinet and pulls the metal head free, making it ready for use. Waking down the corridor with the spear waving in front of her, the bristle end is just behind her back, and she has to keep twisting it so the flat end doesn't catch on her hips when she pushes the bladed end forward.

She stops at the first door, listens quietly, and only when she is sure there is no noise does she try the handle. *No knocking this time*, she tells herself – *move silently and do nothing to draw attention to yourself*. All the doors on the 13th floor are locked and secure. Sarah was surprised when she discovered the apartment block had a thirteenth floor; a lot of developers still go straight from twelve to fourteen – out of superstition. Sarah descends each floor in turn – each time she unlocks the fire hose and pulls the head free in preparation. At the 9th floor, she listens at the first door, hears nothing, and tries the door handle. Moving on, she listens and tries the door handles for each door. At the last one, she pauses for a second as she holds the handle down, resting her head against the door. The tension, fear, and concentration are exhausting, and she rolls her shoulders to ease the pain building across them.

'Who's there?' a voice says softly from the other side of the door, and Sarah opens her eyes wide, suddenly very fearful and not wanting to release the handle – in case it gives her away – then she realises the stupidity of this thought process.

'Hello?' the voice calls again, a soft male voice full of fear.

Sarah releases the handle and steps to the side, not wanting the person on the other side to see her trough the peephole.

'I saw you move, who is it?' the voice asks, still soft and very scared.

'I live on …' she pauses, not wanting to give away her floor.

'I live on the 18th floor, I was looking for other people and food,'

The Undead Day Five

she says softly, still not wanting to draw too much attention to her location.

'Are you alone?' the voice asks.

'Yes,' she replies. Sarah hears the sounds of the locks being rotated, bolts and chains being removed and pulled back. The door slowly opens and a man comes into view.

'Hello … Charlie,' Sarah says to the battered and bruised face of the wine bar owner, and he smiles through swollen lips.

ANOTHER BLAND AND BORING VILLAGE, another horde, and again we stop the Saxon well back from them, the engine switched off to save precious fuel.

The crowd are gathered at the front of some shops on the main road.

'Don't they get bored?' I ask Dave.

'I don't think so,' he replies.

'It doesn't look like they're focussed on anything specific, does it? They're all just aimless.'

'Yes, Mr. Howie.'

'I reckon about thirty or so?'

'Twenty-eight.'

'Oh, okay … so, what is it this time? Rocket launchers? Flame throwers? Or are we going for samurai swords?'

'Sniper rifle,' Dave says and gets out of the Saxon to walk around the rear of the vehicle.

'Of course it is, why wouldn't it be? I didn't even know we had a sniper rifle,' I mutter to myself as I climb down. The recruits have piled out and are stretching in the sun and chatting quietly.

Dave comes out of the back doors holding a long bag which he places on the ground, then unzips the full-length zip. He removes a long, green-coloured rifle. The stock is folded and Dave pulls it out to its full-length and then fixes on a long tube to the end of the barrel. He checks the magazine and fixes it to the bottom of the rifle; finally he walks over to the middle of the road and lies down, facing towards the horde.

'This is a L115A3 long-range rifle. The scope is a standard day scope which increases the magnification by 25. There are five rounds in the magazine. The weapon has an adjustable bi-pod so the rifle can be settled while you locate the target. This bit here is a cheek piece …'

'What does that do?' Tucker interrupts him to groans from the rest of the recruits.

'You rest your cheek on it,' Dave answers without expression. He waits for a moment, then goes on.

'The suppressor at the front reduces the range, but it also reduces the noise and flash, which thereby serves to keep the sniper concealed and increase his survivability.' Dave pauses to extend the bi-pod and make minor adjustments, as he looks through the scope towards the gathered horde.

They have noticed our arrival and have turned to shuffle towards us, but the distance means it will take them quite a long time to get near us. I keep my assault rifle ready, just in case any of them decide to start sprinting.

'The rifle fires an 8.59 millimetre round; this is heavier than some sniper rifles, but it means the round is less likely to be deflected over long ranges. The range is six-hundred metres for a solid strike, but it will fire over one kilometre and still be effective.'

The recruits murmur at this, and I'm shocked too at the great distance this thing can cover.

'So, we settle down and breath nice and slowly so we are not jerky. Each movement is slow and controlled. You have to take into account wind speed, but in weather like this and over this distance, that is not an issue. Locate your target and keep your breathing controlled. When you are ready, you squeeze the trigger, do not snatch at it as you will jerk the rifle and ruin your aiming. Squeeze and fire.' The rifle makes a coughing noise and I watch a head explode in the middle of the horde as the body drops down amongst them.

'Okay, Mr. Howie, would you like to try?' Dave asks me.

The Undead Day Five

'I'll try, mate, but you know what I was like with that last rifle.' I go over and drop down to lie flat. I snuggle my shoulder into the end of the stock and rest my cheek on the cheek piece. I always thought that you put your eye right against the scope, but Dave shows me to look through it and locate the target. I choose a fat one, front centre. His head is wobbling less than the others, due to his fat neck.

'Breath gently, identify the target, and move slowly to make adjustments if you need to,' Dave instructs. 'When you are ready, squeeze the trigger.'

I keep the head in sight. It sways from left to right and I keep focussed on the middle of the sway, breathe slowly, and squeeze the trigger.

The end coughs and I watch as the head explodes and the bullet rips through, taking the back of the skull off and going into the chest of another zombie behind the fat one. They both fall down and the recruits cheer and applaud as I get back to my feet.

'You got two, well done, sir,' McKinney says and the rest join in.

I grin back at them and Tucker hands me my rifle.

'I'll go up on the GPMG while you take your turns,' I say to them, then climb in through the back and up through the hole. I check all around to make sure there aren't any sneaky ninja zombies trying to creep up on us. Dave settles each recruit and goes through the same instructions as he did for me. Blowers first, then Cookey; Tucker struggles, due to his larger size, and just pulls the trigger quickly and gets up. Reese goes next and lies down next to the rifle. He calmly settles himself down and stays still for long seconds, making very minor adjustments. He hardly seems to move and, even from this close distance, I cannot see him breathing. He takes the shot and the round strikes centre forehead, taking the back of the head off in an explosion of blood and brains. He'd aimed for one of the undead at the rear of the group, deliberately choosing a more difficult target. The lads all cheer for Reese and he responds by going bright red.

'Try another one,' Dave says, as Reese starts getting up. He nods and settles back down.

'That one at the back – the small woman in the pink thing,' Dave says.

I look over and see a small-built zombie woman at the rear of the group. She is shuffling the same as the rest, but her head is wobbling quickly and erratically.

Reese settles and pauses for long seconds, then squeezes the trigger. The woman drops immediately with her head blown apart.

'Fucking good shot, mate,' Cookey says and bends down to pat Reese on the back.

'That was very good mate, well done,' Blowers says. Reese blushes even more as Dave watches him closely.

'Let him do another one,' McKinney calls out, and the others all shout in agreement.

'Okay, I want you to take the one on the far right with the white shorts, and then the naked one on the far left,' Dave says. 'But I want them both shot within ten seconds of each other.'

Reese nods and identifies both targets through the scope, sweeping from right to left then back again. He aims for the zombie male on the right with the white shorts and takes the shot. The zombie drops, as before, and Reese racks the bolt and sweeps over to the left and pauses just for a couple of seconds, then takes the second shot. This one strikes her in the mouth, and the zombie gets thrown backwards as the bullet explodes through the back of the skull.

'Sorry, I missed the second one,' Reese says apologetically as he stands up.

'You rushed, and sliding the bolt threw you off a little,' Dave says to him.

I'm amazed at the criticism; two headshots like that were amazing – but Reese nods at Dave.

'Yeah, it felt rushed. I adjusted my position as I reached for the bolt and I didn't need to,' Reese explains. Dave allows the rest of the recruits a go. Nearly all of them miss head shots, and they all seem flat after Reese's amazing efforts.

'Jamie, you finish them off,' Dave says to Reese as the rest of them stand back.

The Undead Day Five

Reese nods quietly and goes to drop down.

'Go on top of the Saxon,' Dave tells him, and Reese obliges in silence as he clambers up and the rifle is passed to him. I drop down from the GPMG hole and climb out to join the others.

'I will number them for you, starting from the front and always moving from right to left as they go back, got it?' Dave calls up.

'Got it,' Reese affirms, quietly.

'Front centre, large-built male is one; two is the female with blonde hair; three is the old man in the striped pyjamas …' Dave continues to count them out, showing Reese his method of selecting multiple targets.

'Ready?' Dave calls.

'Yes,' Reese replies softly.

Dave waits a few seconds, then calls out 'ONE.'

Reese takes the shot and the large built zombie drops.

Dave calls out 'TWO,' and the blonde undead gets blown away.

Dave calls out 'FIVE,' and Reese instantly adjusts to identify the target and drops it.

Dave keeps going, calling out random numbers.

Reese only gets one wrong, but all of them are headshots.

There is utter silence, apart from the numbers being called out and the coughing noise from the rifle.

The last one drops to an outburst of loud cheering and clapping from all of us. Even Dave claps and smiles at Reese as he gets down.

'Very good,' Dave says to him simply, and I see Reese swell with pride from the praise.

'So, we have a sniper in the team,' I say to Reese and shake his hand.

He looks down, clearly uncomfortable.

'Right, let's get loaded and gone from here, time is ticking and we need fuel,' I call out, and the lads all load up. I get into the driver's seat and look across as Blowers gets into the passenger seat.

'Dave is showing Jamie how to strip and clean the rifle, so you've got me for a bit, Mr. Howie,'

'Okay mate, no worries.' I start the engine and we pull away, driving straight over the bodies and crushing them into the road.

The country roads give way to more urban areas and, despite the fuel getting lower, I keep the speed up as we drive through the towns. The signs of devastation and severe civil uproar are everywhere, just like in Portsmouth: burnt-out cars and vehicles, shop fronts smashed in, and bodies everywhere. Some of the houses have been burnt out too, and there more signs of fire-damaged buildings the deeper we go.

Dave has swapped with Blowers now and is sitting up front with me again. Curtis Graves is on the GPMG, and the rest of them stay quiet. The villages were quaint, but we didn't really see signs of just how severe the outbreak is. But here is different, it's gritty and it reminds me that a whole lot of people live in this country and every single one of them has been deeply affected by this event. The tragedy is everywhere, in the roads and streets, in the smashed-in buildings with their front doors hanging open. Bloodstains and smears are all over the road and on road signs and metal railings. The bodies that we see are festering and already rapidly decaying in the hot summer sun.

'We'll take the motorway into London,' I say to Dave.

'Okay, Mr. Howie.'

The road leads us through the centre of the town, and we see the high street stores have been looted; debris and everyday items litter the ground. There are very few undead though, just a couple here and there, shuffling along and slowly turning to watch us as we drive past. A man runs out in front of the road ahead of us, waving his arms and shouting loudly. I didn't see where he came from, although it must have been from one of the shops or buildings. I slow the vehicle down and he stays in the middle of the road, trying to stop us with his physical presence. I slow to a full stop with him standing just a few feet in front of us. He walks around to my side and looks up as I open the window slightly.

'Thank God, I knew the Army would come,' the man shouts. He is middle-aged and dressed in suit trousers and an office-style shirt, now filthy with grime.

'We're not the Army, mate, we're just using this vehicle,' I say to him.

The Undead Day Five

'Well … you've got a man on the top with a machine gun,' he shouts back.

'Er … well yes, but we're just trying to get somewhere.'

'You have to help. I got trapped trying to get supplies and I can't get back to my family. I tried to go back but they're surrounded by those things!' the man shouts in desperation and indicates a side street; tears are streaming down his face and he looks petrified.

I glance over to Dave, who shrugs his shoulders.

'How far away are they?' I ask him. I don't want to keep stopping, but he's clearly desperate.

'Down there, not far, honestly, just down there.' He moves quickly from foot to foot, pointing back to the side street off to the left.

'Okay, hop on the ledge and direct us.'

The man climbs up, holding onto the wing mirror and balancing on the driver's step. I drive forward and the man keeps waving to the side street and shouting:

'… down there, down there.'

I turn in and drive down the road for a few hundred metres.

'Down this road.' The man waves to a residential street and I see a handful of undead immediately outside a terraced house.

'Bloody hell, mate – there's only a few of 'em – I thought you said there were loads.'

'There is loads, look at them, I'll never get through them,'

'Are you being serious?' I look at the man incredulously.

'What? How am I supposed to get through them!' he cries.

'What about weapons? You must have armed yourself.'

'Well, I've never really believed in violence, and I don't like weapons,' he says defensively.

'Oh, but it's all right for us to use our weapons?' I shout at him.

'But you're the Army …'

'We are *not* the bloody Army,' I cut across him. 'You are not going to survive very long without weapons and being willing to bloody use them.'

'But …' he tries to stammer.

'No *but's* mate – you said you have a family in there – kids and a wife?'

he nods.

'So *man up* and defend your family.' I push the door open and he falls off the ledge. I take my axe and walk towards the five zombies that are shuffling around his front door. The recruits are bursting out of the Saxon and running towards us with their knives, and Dave is already at my side as I walk up to the closest one and behead him as he turns round.

I follow through with the swing and take another one down. Dave has already dropped the other three by the time the recruits get close, and they all stop, looking disappointed, and slowly turn and walk back towards the vehicle. The man is staring open-mouthed at Dave and I, and then at the bloodied bodies on the ground.

'What's up mate, was that too violent for you?' I say as I walk past him to the Saxon.

We drive back up the side streets onto the main road; I glance back once in the mirror and he's still standing there, gaping, his arms hanging at his sides.

We enter the featureless and empty motorway and keep driving towards London. We have no satellite navigation, just a road atlas. Getting into London will be easy enough, apart from the millions of zombies, but finding where my sister lives will be extremely hard.

At least we don't have to worry about one-way roads, no entry signs, or traffic build-ups now, and we won't have to pay the London congestion charge. Mind you, I imagine there will still be someone sat in their offices, clocking the vehicles and sending out letters to their home addresses. A city the size of London should have lots of survivors holed up, so maybe they have already started cutting the numbers of zombies down.

That radio message said that London was infected and to stay away, but that was a few days ago now. I imagine driving through an empty city centre, with piles of zombie bodies stacked up neatly, ready to be burnt.

It won't be like that, but a man is allowed to dream.

The Undead Day Five

'There's some services on this road,' Curtis Graves calls out.

'Thanks mate, how do you know that? I guess you've been here before then?'

'We used to go to 4x4 vehicle shows and take our old Land Rover. Dad always worked out each service station, so we could stop, if it broke down,' Graves says.

'And did it break down?'

'Rarely. They tend to go on forever, especially the old ones – you just need a few tools and a working knowledge and they are easy to fix.'

'How far up this road, mate?' I say, looking down at the fuel gauge that is now only a little bit above the red line.

'Only a few miles, not far.'

'Do any of you know how to get fuel out when there is no power?' I shout.

'I know they either have to press a button inside the kiosk to allow the fuel out, or it's done on an automated system when the cameras have had time to record the registration number,' Nick Hewitt shouts down to me.

'What about now – with no power in the service station?'

'I don't know, but some of the main services have to have backup generators in case of power outages, so they can still get fuel to the emergency services and stuff,' Hewitt shouts.

'Curtis, is this service station a large one?' I ask him.

'Yes, sir – it's the only one for quite a while.'

'Okay, we'll aim for that then. We have to get fuel and Dave has experience with generators.' I cast him a glance as I remember him electrifying the metal gates outside the police station.

'Dave and Curtis, can you two go for the generator? Nick, I want you to try and find out how to activate the pumps, if we manage to get the power back on. Darren, you take the GPMG and Jamie, go up-top with the sniper rifle. The rest of us will spread out and keep watch, got it?'

I get a chorus of YESES from behind me. I glance over and see Dave staring at me, and, although his face is blank, I can tell he is thinking of something.

'What?' I ask him.

'Nothing, Mr. Howie.'

'Was that a bad plan? Change it if you want to, mate – sorry, I should have checked with you first.'

'It's a good plan.' He looks back to the front.

'It is a very good plan.'

Chapter 11

Sarah stands in the apartment's entryway with the front door directly behind her, staring at Charlie – her makeshift spear is lowered but is still pointing towards him, and he keeps glancing nervously at the large blade taped to the end.

'I didn't know you lived here, too?' Charlie says.

'Or you,' Sarah says.

'You been here long?' he asks.

'A little while.' She watches him gingerly touch his bruised and battered face. His lips are still swollen and the bruising has gone a sickening shade of yellow.

'It still hurts,' he moans.

'Does it?' Although this is the first person she has seen in days, Sarah is not overwhelmed with joy to see the sleazy bar owner.

'So where is your wife?' she asks.

'Err … I haven't seen her for a few days,' he mumbles quietly and looks away.

'Doesn't she live here with you?' she asks him, puzzled.

'Err, well she did, kind of.' He looks very uncomfortable.

'You left her there, when all this was happening? You left her on her own?' she demands, her voice rising slightly.

'Well, it was all going mad and someone had to stay and lock up. I needed to get changed after that crazy man attacked me for no reason.'

'That crazy man was the husband of a woman you groped, I'm surprised it didn't happen a long time ago,' Sarah shouts.

'What woman?' a tall girl with long, straight black hair asks. She has a slight accent.

'Oh, hello,' Sarah says, surprised.

'Hello. What woman?' she repeats.

'I'm Sarah, nice to meet you,' Sarah says.

'Hello Sarah, I'm Vivien.' The woman is strikingly beautiful with high cheekbones, but with a surly, pouty face.

'What woman?'

Vivien looks to Charlie and then back at Sarah. Charlie visibly squirms under her gaze.

'Excuse me, Vivien, I don't mean to be rude – but Charlie was just telling me how he left his wife at the bar when all of this happened …'

'Not my problem,' Vivien shrugs.

'He left her to die,' Sarah says, shocked at the coldness of the woman.

'Like I said, not my problem,' Vivien says again, pouting.

'So, how did you get here?' Sarah asks the woman.

'Charlie got me from the hotel on Friday night,' she replies expressionlessly.

'The hotel?' Sarah asks.

'I was staying in a hotel near here. Charlie came and got me and we came here.'

'You fucking scum, you left your wife to die and went to get your girlfriend instead?' Sarah shouts at Charlie.

'I didn't know what was happening. I was coming home to get changed and picked Vivien up on the way …'

'You were beaten up for groping another woman, and then, when the whole world erupts, you slink off to get your mistress from the hotel she is hiding in – to have a quickie at home?' Sarah shouts loudly now, gripping the spear hard.

The Undead Day Five

'What woman? You said there was a fight at the bar!' Vivien shouts at Charlie, erupting in anger.

'You fucking cunt, you said there was a fight – but a man beat you up for grabbing his wife? You dirty, fucking animal!' Vivien screams, her accent getting stronger with the instant rage.

Sarah stares in shock at the sudden outburst.

Vivien turns and walks into the bedroom and slams the door. She re-opens it a few seconds later and stands there with her arms folded.

'You fucker. You got me in a hotel waiting for you, and your wife at home, and you were touching some other woman? You disgust me. Filthy fucker!' Vivien shouts, her face contorted with anger.

'No, Viv – I didn't. I promise I didn't, it was all wrong – just some mad bloke,' Charlie pleads with her.

'You can fuck off with your promises, you make empty promises, always empty promises …'

'Viv, please …' he looks at her pleadingly.

'I gave up a life for you, a home with a decent man; I gave up my job and my studies and got into debt. I had a life and you promised me you would take care of me. I even had to pay my own fucking hotel bill – you cheap dirty man ….'

'Err … excuse me, have you seen what's going on out there?' Sarah interjects.

'I don't fucking care!' Vivien screams.

'Well I do, as far as we know the whole world has fallen. That creep left his own wife to die and now you're arguing about him touching up another woman …'

'Who the fuck are you to talk to me, don't talk to me – you fucking whore, you're all whores in this country!' Vivien screams, the veins in her neck bulging out, and suddenly she isn't so beautiful.

'Okay, listen Vivien, those *things* are in the building, and if you don't keep your voice down, they will come here.' Sarah says, with a firm, level voice.

'This is your fault,' Vivien turns back to Charlie. 'This is all your fault, you fucking prick, and now we're going to die in this shithole.'

'Now listen to me, you bitch. You made your choice and now it's too late, so don't fucking moan at me …' Charlie retorts in anger.

'What!? I'm moaning, am I – you promised me a life and this is what I get? You cheap, bloody man.'

'Viv, you're a cheap bitch that fell for it, that's your fault, what did you expect from me? I'm fucking married, for God's sake.'

Vivien runs across the room and starts pummelling his body and face with her fists, her long black hair flying about.

Sarah slowly backs away, fearing the loud noise will draw the zombies there. She quietly opens the front door and checks the corridor, then pulls the door closed behind her. The sound of the raised voices and glass smashing can still be heard as Sarah reaches the stairwell and quickly goes down to the next level.

The noise will draw those things, but it will also mask any noise she makes, so she moves quickly onto the next level, trying door handles and then thinking to check under the floor mats. The next couple of floors are all locked and secure, but then she gets lucky and finds a shiny key under a mat outside a door. She quietly listens and then slides the key in, gently pushing the door open. Once again, the apartment is a replica of hers – the layout and the room sizes are the same, just the décor is different. She eases forward slowly, making each step land softly and shifting her weight from foot to foot. The lounge is clear. She checks the bedroom and bathroom which are also empty, and breathes a sigh of relief as she rushes into the kitchen and checks through the cupboards. The various tinned goods get swept into a bag that she finds in a drawer, plus some rice cakes and unopened cartons of orange juice. Within minutes, she is back outside and replaces the key under the mat, just in case the owner returns and, also, in case she gets stuck away from her apartment again.

Back in the stairwell, she climbs up and pauses when she reaches Charlie and Vivien's floor. She slowly peeks through the door and her heart sinks as she watches the zombie shuffle along the corridor, towards the still raised voices.

Sarah shakes her head at the blind stupidity of it all and begins making her way back to her own apartment. On the next floor up, she has to dart back down and hide as a zombie shuffles through the door and into the stairwell; the slow and heavy footsteps resound on the carpet as the cumbersome thing drops down each step. The zombie moves slowly and Sarah keeps backing further down, staying out of sight, until the zombie follows the sound of the voices and enters the corridor.

Sarah wastes no time and quickly sprints up the stairs until she reaches her own floor, where she checks that it is empty. Then she runs back into the safety of her own apartment, heady with the sense of victory at the accomplished mission and the gained supplies.

WE DRIVE QUICKLY DOWN the slip road to the services, following the long, narrow route until we reach a fork in the road. I take the right path and drive into a service station. Several rows of fuel pumps with green and black handles are stretched across the centre. The pumps on the far end look bigger, and I guess they are for commercial-sized vehicles; I aim for those pumps and stop before I reach them.

'Which side is the fuel cap on?' I ask Dave and he jumps out and checks both sides.

'Your side,' he shouts up.

'Cheers, mate.' I slide the Saxon alongside the pumps, while Dave waves me forward and then holds his hand up.

'Okay lads, let's go,' I shout out and the rear doors are thrown open. The recruits pile out. Curtis runs to Dave and they both set off towards the rear of the building, carrying their assault rifles at the ready. Darren Smith is already up-top on the GPMG, and I watch Jamie clamber up with the sniper rifle and then start sweeping the area through the scope. Blowers then directs Cookey, Tucker, and McKinney to take a side each. They respond quickly and spread out. I watch them rack their bolts back and make ready. Within seconds, everyone is where they should be and I glance over to see Nick Hewitt trying to force the doors open.

'Is it locked?' I shout to Nick.

'Yep, locked up tight,' he calls back.

'Fuck, I wasn't expecting that. I can't believe it's still locked and hasn't been looted yet,' I join him at the electric doors, which are shut tight and secure.

'I'll get the axe, hang on.' I run to and from the Saxon and then I take a big swing and strike the glass in the middle, holding my head away to avoid any flying glass. The axe has dented the glass but that's it. I strike again and again but the glass holds tight.

'Security glass,' I say to Nick. 'Try shooting it.'

I step back and turn round to face the other direction.

'NICK IS GOING TO SHOOT THE DOORS,' I call out, so the others don't panic when they hear the shots. Nick aims and fires once; the round makes a hole in the glass pane, but otherwise, no damage. I use the axe to strike at the bullet hole, hoping it has weakened the structure, but it holds fast.

'Fuck this, hang on mate.' I run back to the Saxon, climb into the back, and start checking through the various storage sections until I find a nice long, thick chain – with a hook on one end. I find a hole at the bottom front of the Saxon and attach one end of the chain, then stretch it across to the doors and wind it through the bar handles several times. Once back in the Saxon, I engage the reverse gear and the chain pulls tight. I apply slightly more pressure to the gas; the doors are pulled clean off and get dragged a few feet until I stop and drive back to where we were. Hewitt runs straight into the shop area and I see him make for the counter. Curtis comes running round to the front, towards me.

'We've got it ready, it should be on in a minute or so, sir,' he yells as he gets closer.

'Well done mate, we just need Nick to figure out how to turn the pumps on now.'

Chapter 12

The infection has tracked the group through the countryside and then watched them trundling through the towns.

Each host turns to watch the distinctive vehicle as it drives past them.

Then they stopped and took down more hosts. It watched the one they call Howie using that long implement and the other smaller one cutting the throats and causing the precious lifeblood to drain away within seconds. The infection had watched them as the smaller one spoke to the others and then they all used sharp implements to cut through host necks. Then they stopped again and used another tool to blow the heads off. The infection watched and waited, tracking their movements, and sent the rats out in that area to find them, stop them, and kill them. The rats hunt and watch. The eyes are different than the human hosts, but the sight is still excellent and the infection watches through hundreds of thousands of eyes, just waiting for them to reappear.

⸻

'FUCKING LOOK at the size of that rat!' Cookey shouts, and we all turn to see a big, fat black rat sitting on the top of a waste bin, off to the side of the fuel station.

'That's fatter than you, Tucker,' McKinney shouts.

'Fuck off, we like our food – don't we, my lovely,' Tucker shouts towards the rat.

'Argh, they're disgusting, I fucking hate rats,' Blowers says.

'Must be full up from chomping on all of those bodies,' Tucker says, with gruesome relish.

'Ah … Tucker, that's fucking gross, you dirty bastard,' Cookey shouts at him. I watch the rat watching us. There is no fear in it and I guess that they have evolved and gotten braver.

'That fucking thing is watching us,' Blowers says with disgust.

'Jamie, do you think you could hit that rat from up there?' I shout over to him. He nods and lies down on top of the Saxon, aiming towards the litter bin.

I hear a slight cough and the rat is blown apart in a burst of pink and black fur. We all cheer and Jamie gives a slight nod and carries on scanning the area.

'He's morphing into Dave,' I mutter under my breath.

THE INFECTION WATCHES the group and the one they call Howie walking back and forth. The smaller one has gone out of sight, but they are all holding those long things that kill the hosts so easily.

The rat sits and watches the group, fully controlled by the infection as it takes in the area; the rat is made to piss down the sides of the waste bin so that others can track its location. Another one pops its head out from some bushes further back and watches the rat on the waste bin.

Then another one climbs out of a drain cover and watches the one in the bushes.

More start popping out all around the area, watching the others and marking the site, pissing where they stand so that the infection can use their powerful sense of smell. Within minutes, there are rats throughout the fuel station site. Their red eyes almost glow against the darkness of their fur. The scent markers work, and rats from miles around are sent surging towards the location. A scent trail is laid by each rat as it gets closer to the smells left by the preceding rodents. Survivors fighting for their lives against the rats invading their homes are suddenly dumbfounded when the rats turn as one and start running away. They look out of *their windows and peek holes to see a thick carpet of black bodies all running in one direction. The motorway that Howie and the recruits used just a short time ago is slowly filling with sleek black bodies and fat black bodies – first in ones, then twos, then small groups – until they are piling in from the sides, the drain covers – all pushing towards one direction. Slowly, the infection is able to watch the group from many different eyes, but it holds the rats back, and waits. The infection has learnt to resist the urge to send these small hosts in; it must wait until there are enough to overwhelm them.*

'GOT IT,' Nick Hewitt bellows from behind the counter.

'Well done mate, nice one,' I say from the end of the aisle.

I had just taken cans of warm drinks out to the lads, carrying them in a basket and letting them select the ones they wanted. Then, while I was waiting for Dave and Nick to figure out how to get the power supply to switch to the generator, I stocked up the back of the Saxon with more chocolate bars and snacks.

The room suddenly fills with light, and the chilled cabinets start up with a clunk and a whirl. The pumps outside make a noise, and I watch the lads all turn to look at them and start smiling.

'Is the pump ready, Nick?' I ask him.

'Um, hang on sir, I'm just figuring it out.'

'How do you know about these things? Have you worked in fuel stations before?'

'No sir, I just like technology and electrical stuff, computers, that kind of thing. I love figuring out how stuff works.'

'Oh right, I thought all of you were unemployed?'

'We were – I was.'

'How come, if you can do this kind of thing? There must have been employers out there desperate for blokes like you.'

'I'm dyslexic, sir.' He looks up at me with a grin.

'The Army was going to help with that … well, they were going to … anyway.'

'Bloody hell, didn't they do that at school?'

'Not really, they thought I was pissing around and just not trying and, by the time they figured it out, it was too late really and I lost interest. I was bunking off all the time. Oh ... here we are, right ... that should be it.'

'Have you done it?'

'I think so. Try it now and give me a shout if it doesn't work,' he says as I leave the store and cross to the pumps.

I unwind the fuel cap and sniff the hole, just to be sure it's diesel and not petrol. I wouldn't have thought these things would run on petrol, that would cost a fortune, but after the last time we put the wrong fuel in I double check. I press the lever in on the black handle and feel the vibration as it starts to pump fuel into the tank. I give a thumbs up back to Nick, who returns the gesture and starts walking out from behind the counter. Then he stops and goes back and slides up the metal shutter that hides the cigarette display. He looks over at me, gesturing towards the tobacco display. From his manner it appears he is asking if it's okay to take some cigarettes.

Bless him; he doesn't have to ask me.

I give him another thumbs up and nod vigorously, showing that I don't mind. The fuel pumps steadily into the tank as I watch Nick load up bags with all of the cigarettes, tobacco, papers, and lighters, and stroll back outside.

He goes over to the lads and shows them the contents and I'm surprised when Blowers, Cookey, and McKinney all take a packet and light up.

Tucker declines and walks over to the Saxon, as Dave walks back around from behind the building with Curtis.

'Do want you a packet, sir?' Nick asks me.

'Nah ... you're all right, mate. I gave up a little while ago, would be a shame to start now – right at the end of the world.'

'Okay, lads do you want any smokes?' Nick calls up to Jamie and Darren on top of the Saxon.

'Yeah ... I will in a minute, mate. Best not smoke here with all this fuel about,' Darren calls down.

'Probably a good idea,' I say.

'Is it okay if I go over to the side for a smoke, sir?' Nick asks me.

'Yeah, mate, no problem.'

The Undead Day Five

Dave walks up and watches the fuel handle. Curtis joins Nick Hewitt and Blowers chatting away and takes a packet of cigarettes, opens it up and lights one. They all stand chatting, blowing smoke into the air, and I notice they keep their observations up and are constantly scanning the area.

'Fuck me, they nearly all smoke,' I say to Dave.

'Squaddies, Mr. Howie – they nearly all smoke.'

'I thought soldiers had to be super fit.'

'There's a difference between being fit and being healthy.'

'Have you ever smoked, Dave?'

'No, Mr. Howie.'

'I used to, but I gave up. Watching them now makes me want one though.'

'Are you going to have one?' he asks me.

'God no, far too expensive. I can't afford them anymore.'

'True, they do cost a lot,' Dave answers, missing the joke.

'Or you could just sign for them, seeing as you're a manager ...' he says, *not* missing the joke.

'Bloody hell, Dave ... did you just make a joke?' I ask him, shocked at his reference to when I met up with him in the supermarket and tried to get him to take some clean clothes from the clothing section. He had refused, saying he had no money and I told him I would sign for them.

Dave just gives a slight smile, but his eyes are glinting.

'Well mate, you *are* changing. Becoming an instructor, smiling and even making jokes now, I just don't recognise you anymore, you've changed – you're not the person I met.' I smile at him. He looks puzzled and stares at me.

'I am,' he says.

'I was just joking, mate.'

'Oh, okay.'

'SIR!' Jamie Reese shouts out loudly from his position above us on the Saxon.

'What's up, Jamie?' I lean back to look up at him, but he is facing the other way.

'Sir ... There are lots of rats all around us.' Reese says.

'Rats? I wouldn't worry mate, they're just getting brave now that all the people are gone.'

'I don't think so, sir. Maybe you should look.' He sounds concerned and I get Dave to hold the pump lever down, while I clamber up-top.

'Where, mate?' I ask him, once I'm next to him.

'Everywhere, sir, have a look,' he says. I take the rifle and look through the scope. I scan quickly from left to right.

'You're too high, sir, look down to the bottom of the bushes – at the edge of the car park,' Jamie says.

I can just see the top of the main services building, where the shops and cafés are. I lower down to the bushes. As I focus and watch, I see black shapes emerging and then staying still. I sweep along the bottom of the bushes and can see hundreds and hundreds of rats, all looking in our direction. I keep sweeping and see more emerging every few seconds, and my heart misses a beat as I notice their small, beady, red eyes.

Zombie eyes.

Zombie rats.

They don't move though, but just squat still, watching all of us.

'Everyone ... back in the Saxon right now – but do not run,' I shout out.

I hear footsteps as the lads all start heading back, all of them quiet, and I can tell by the noise they are walking fast.

The pump switches off as Dave extracts the nozzle and I hear the clunk as he rests it back on the stand. More and more rats are coming into the perimeter, and I sweep the scope over to the access road and almost shout out when I see a thick black carpet of undulating bodies sweeping towards us.

'Smith, get that gun aimed on the access road leading in, is everyone loaded up?' I shout down.

'Apart from you and Jamie yes – what's going on?' I hear Blowers say.

'Lads, there are thousands of rats watching us and more are coming. They are wild zombie rats. Jamie, I want you to get back

The Undead Day Five

inside, mate.' I hear movement as Jamie drops down to the rear and climbs into the back.

'Smith, you drop down, mate – I'll take the machine gun. Curtis, can you hear me?'

'Yes, sir,' Graves replies.

'Get up front, into the driver's seat, and get us out of here,' I say, trying to keep my voice level and calm. I glance over and see that Darren Smith has dropped back down.

I lower the sniper rifle and ease myself into the hole and take over the GPMG.

I pull the lever back and aim directly at the entrance to the access road. Movement catches my eye and I look over to the shop area. The fuel pumps are covered by a large, flat roof to keep customers dry when they are filling up. The store building also has a flat roof – only inches away from the edge of the fuel pump roof. Black bodies are running and jumping onto the fuel pump area roof.

'Shit, they're above us – quick, Curtis, get us out of here!' I shout down.

The engine starts and I hear Curtis grinding the gears as he tries to select first. Then I hear skittering noises directly above me as the rats' tiny claws scratch against the top of the metal roof. I look back to the hedgerow just as thousands of rats burst out and start running directly towards us. More are coming from the other side and, within seconds, the ground is covered by the rodents as they surge forward.

'NOW, CURTIS!' I bellow, and then realise that if I open up with the GPMG I run the risk of hitting the fuel pumps which would blow us all sky high. The Saxon starts forward and rolls away from the fuel area. The rats are already close to the vehicle and I move around in a circle to see them come from all directions. Curtis increases his speed and turns to go back down the access road which we came up. The tyres start hitting the rats and I hear popping noises and crunches as they are squashed under the giant wheels.

'KEEP GOING,' I yell, and wait until we are clear of the fuel pumps before opening up with the GPMG.

The rats' bodies are small, but there are so many of them that I can't see the road surface now. The heavy calibre machine gun rips through them, sending bodies flying into the air. But for every rat that is torn apart by the machine gun, several more appear.

I spin around to face back towards the pumps and see them pouring around the sides of the building, all heading our way. Now thousands of rats with red bloodshot eyes surge towards us and, as we clear the end of the flat roof, I see bodies dropping down onto the top of the Saxon.

'FUCK ... THEY'RE ON THE TOP!' I scream out and feel the Saxon give a burst of speed as Curtis tries to shake them off.

Several of them fall off, but a few remain and start walking towards me, rocking with the motion of the vehicle. I can't shoot them, as I don't know if the rounds will penetrate the armoured vehicle from this close range, and the gun won't aim down that low anyway.

I open fire on the fuel station and pour rounds into ground level.

Bodies get burst apart and blown away and I see mini-explosions of blood as the large bullets rip through their bodies. I keep firing and the rounds hit the fuel pumps; I aim for the one we were using. As we get onto the access road and are crushing hundreds of rats beneath us, the fuel pump explodes into flames with a massive bang. Thick, black smoke billows up and rolls across the flat roof and over the sides. The fuel in the pipes gets set alight and, within seconds, the other pumps are exploding, sending scorched bits of rat bodies past me from the pressure wave.

Each pump goes with a massive *BANG* and a huge fireball erupts upwards, incinerating the flat roof within seconds. The structure collapses from the sudden, intense heat which sends more flames and smoke billowing out the sides. Another huge fireball explodes and this one is much bigger than the previous; the remains of the roof are launched high into the sky – jagged chunks of metal flying off in different directions.

One large chunk is sent wheeling through the air, directly at us, and I drop down just as it bounces off the rear and goes spinning over us – landing directly in the path of the Saxon.

The Undead Day Five

Curtis slams the brakes on and we all go flying forward, then off to the side as he steers around the obstacle.

'There's fucking thousands of them,' I shout out above the noise of the engine screaming and the huge explosions behind us.

Just as I move back towards the GPMG hole, a big, fat black rat drops down onto the floor of the Saxon. We all shout and scream and start stamping down with our boots, but the speedy body darts and weaves through us.

Another fat body drops down and now we are trying to stamp down on two of them. Tucker's big boot gets the first one – which explodes under his foot, bits of blood and fur spraying out.

'Fucking got him,' Tucker yells, with victory.

'Get that other fucker then,' Cookey yells, as we keep trying to stamp down and kick it. The rat is darting about very fast and trying to leap up at our legs, the long yellow teeth bared and gnashing with ferociousness.

'Yeah, got both of the fuckers,' Tucker yells as his massive boot crushes the next one.

'Thank fuck for that, I fucking hate rats.' Blowers sinks back onto the bench seat just as several more rats drop down from the hole and start running around the back.

'CURTIS – WE HAVE TO STOP!' I shout out, as we all dance up and down, stamping our feet.

'THEY'RE EVERYWHERE THOUGH,' Curtis yells back.

'HEAD FOR THE SERVICES BUILDING, FUCKING QUICKLY TOO.'

We all jolt as the Saxon goes in a straight line and speeds up, bouncing over the kerbs and lane dividers. We keep jumping and slamming our feet down as a rat jumps onto the front of Darren's trousers and starts climbing up his legs, onto his stomach.

Blowers punches out hard and strikes the rat in the middle of its body; the rat drops down but the blow was hard and knocked Darren back onto the benches.

'Sorry mate,' Blowers shouts.

'It's okay,' Darren yells as he gets up, winded, but still dancing on the spot.

'ALMOST THERE, MAKE READY,' Dave bellows at the top of his voice, and we all try to pick our assault rifles and bags up as we bounce up and down, black bodies scurrying and jumping at our boots.

'BRACE,' Dave yells, too late, as Curtis slams the brakes on – bringing the Saxon to a grinding halt.

We all go flying and I drop down onto my hands and knees. A rat launches at my face and is kicked aside by a black boot.

'THANK YOU!' I shout as I get back up, and we all scrabble to get to the back doors, bursting out onto the concrete just a few feet away from the front doors.

'GET INSIDE,' Dave yells and we all start running to the doors. Dave gets there first and slams into them and bounces off.

'LOCKED,' he yells and starts kicking at the doors. I get to his side and glance back to the car park. We have gained a few seconds, but the rats are pouring across the car park. I start hammering on the doors and see someone moving around inside. A man appears, running towards the doors, but stops when he sees several armed and crazy-looking men yelling at him.

'OPEN THE DOORS,' Dave shouts, but the man walks a bit further, then stops and stares back at us – a terrified look on his face. Dave steps back and aims his assault rifle directly at the man.

'I CAN SHOOT YOU FASTER THAN YOU CAN RUN. OPEN THE DOORS NOW.'

The man jerks forward and pulls a set of keys out of his pocket and fumbles with a lock; eventually, he opens the door and we burst in, roughly pushing him aside. We all try to get at the doors at the same time and slam them shut; the keys are still in the lock and I manage to turn them and pull them out just as the rats slam into the glass panes from the other side. We all jump backwards and aim our assault rifles down into the writhing mass.

'DON'T SHOOT, YOU'LL BREAK THE GLASS,' Dave shouts and we all slowly lower our weapons, watching with horror and disgust as the rats throw themselves at the doors.

Several of them stretch their mouths wide open and try to bite at the smooth glass, but all I can see are hundreds and hundreds of pairs of red eyes.

'We need to seal the building up,' I say to the recruits. 'Team Alpha, take the left side with Dave … Team Bravo, the right side with me. Make sure every door and window is closed and locked.'

Dave, McKinney, Smith, Tucker, and Hewitt all run off to the front left side of the building, straight into the café area. To the right is a convenience-style shop, and I start into it with Blowers, Cookey, Reese, and Graves. We sweep around the edge of the building, kicking in doors and shouting clear when we have checked the area.

The convenience store has a storeroom and small staff canteen; both have doors and windows leading to outside, but all are checked and found to be locked securely. We move out of the shop and down the wide central aisle. The next room on the right is a small amusement arcade with darkened fruit machines. I watch the lads quickly sweep the rooms, but the room is sealed internally with no other doors. As they come back out, I hear a woman screaming and see her running out of the restrooms – which are directly ahead of us.

'There's a rat in the toilet,' she screams, and doesn't even take in the armed men walking towards her.

I see a Burger King off to the right, a long counter and seating area with tables and chairs with several people all standing up to look at us.

'There are thousands of rats trying to get inside this building, we need to seal every point of access,' I shout at them, scaring them witless, and a woman faints and falls onto the floor.

A young child starts screaming and is picked up by another adult female.

'Blowers, you check in there with Cookey – Jamie and Curtis with me to the toilets.'

'SIR,' they all shout.

I run ahead to the toilets: one wide access in, the males to the right and the females to the left.

'Jamie, you take the right side, Curtis with me.'

We split up as Curtis and I burst into the ladies' toilet. The first cubicle door is open and a fat, black rat is climbing out of the toilet bowl, using its front paws to pull itself up. I run into the cubicle and slam the lid down hard, crushing the rat dead. I lift the lid and use my foot to push it back inside, then slam the lid down again.

I hear Curtis yelling and slamming the lid down in the next cubicle, and I move out and around to the next one after that. I see one rat already on the floor, scrabbling towards me. I take a running kick and splat it against the rear wall; the body hits, slides down and remains motionless on the floor. The next rat drops out of the bowl onto the ground and I stamp down, crushing the wet, shit-smeared body. I move from cubicle to cubicle, pulverising rats as they appear.

'Curtis, I'll hold these, you find something heavy to put on the lids,' I shout to him. I position myself a few feet back so that I can see all of the cubicles and then run forward to crush or kick them as they appear.

I'm kept busy as they keep coming, until I pick the dirty, wet, dead zombie rat bodies up and throw them into the bowls to try and block them. I keep doing this until each bowl is filled with dead rats, then I put the lids down, but can still hear them fidgeting and moving about. I push the flush buttons for each bowl, trying to drown any living undead rats that are still down there. Curtis bursts in with Blowers and Cookey, each of them carrying a heavy, long, cylindrical waste bin. We put the heavy metal bins on the lids and step back to see if the rats can get out. After a couple of minutes, I am satisfied that they can't, so I push the already dead rats out of the way and get the lid up.

'Burger King is clear, sir,' Blowers says.

'Thanks mate, what about the men's toilets?' I ask Jamie.

'We did the same thing in there, they were trying to come up through the bowls, too.'

'Okay, let's see if the others are all right.' We leave the toilets and make our way into the central area; Dave and Team Alpha are already waiting for us.

'All clear for the minute, Mr. Howie, but it won't last long,' Dave says as we join them. Nick has pulled out a packet of cigarettes and the lads start lighting up, after Nick looks at me for approval.

'Crack on, lads – I think we need a few minutes' rest after that,' I say to them as they light up, taking deep drags.

'I know what you mean, we always had rats in the supermarket; the fuckers will get through anything for food. This place has air-conditioning, so there will be vents. Also, the drains will need sealing up.'

'Okay, Mr. Howie,' Dave says.

'Mr. Howie, are those fucking things zombies too?' Tucker asks me.

'They certainly look like it, mate – I don't plan on getting bitten though – so I cannot be exactly sure, but look at those eyes.'

'Yeah, but why are they coming for us, Mr. Howie?' Smith asks me, and they all look to me for an answer.

'I don't know, but it bloody looked like that, didn't it? They were watching us for ages before they started to attack. There's people here they could have come for, but, mind you, we *were* out in the open and they were locked in here.' I shake my head, trying to make sense of it all.

'What a fucking day,' I add and rub my forehead.

We are all sweating heavily from the hot weather and the frantic exercise we have just done.

'I am parched, they must have some fluids in here, let's look.' I turn and walk, amazed that I have used the word *fluids* instead of saying *drink*. Bloody Dave – he is rubbing off on me.

'Er … Hi,' a voice says meekly, and I look up to see the man who unlocked the doors walking slowly out of the entrance to Burger King.

'Hi, sorry about that. We didn't mean to barge you out of the way like that,' I say to him.

'Cookey, you're on first watch, on the front doors – Hewitt, you watch the toilet entrance – we'll bring you some drinks,' I say to the lads and then walk up to the man and extend my hand.

'Hi, I'm Howie,' I say to him and we shake hands.

'Tom. I was the night manager when this happened. There's quite a few others in here too,' he says, nodding towards Burger King. 'Are you guys the Army?'

'No mate, these lads had just joined up when Dave and I found them at Salisbury. We were there to take that huge vehicle …'

'So … that means you *are* the Army then?' Tom says.

'Well … they are newbies, really, and so am I. Dave is the well-trained one. He was in the Army.'

'But … you're in charge of them?'

'I guess, but they're just lads really, we are on our way to London.'

The man nods at me.

'You'd better come and meet the others,' he says, and I follow him into Burger King. The lads are already behind the counter, going through cupboards and pulling out bottles of water.

'Mr. Howie …' Tucker calls out, and throws a bottle of water over as I go past the counter.

'Cheers, mate.' There are about eight or nine adults in here, plus one small child and a baby. They are all clustered around some tables in the middle. The people look very tired and frightened, and keep glancing over to the lads behind the counter. I realise how terrified they must feel, seeing us all in full action. I nod at the group.

'Hi, I'm Howie – sorry about the noise and bursting in like that, and please excuse the lads; they're just getting a drink. We are not here to hurt anyone, I promise, we're just trying to get away from the thousands of rats that are chasing us.' They all start talking at once, and Tom holds up his hand to quieten them.

'Mark, why don't you go first,' Tom says, indicating a man who is still wearing a smart business suit, although the shirt top button is undone and his tie is pulled down slightly.

Mark stands up and glances round at the others before speaking.

'I think I speak for all of us when I ask just what the hell is going on here?' He has a strong, cultured voice.

'What do you mean?' I say to him, puzzled at the question.

'Well you're the Army, I think we have the right to some answers.'

'We are not the Army … I …'

The Undead Day Five

'... but you are dressed like soldiers and are carrying military assault rifles, plus you are driving around in a tank,' Mark continues.

'APC,' the lads chorus.

'Yes, I know how it must look. Dave was in the Army and we are wearing Army clothes, as ours were covered in blood.'

'So, just who are you and why are you here?' Mark demands.

'I'm Howie, that's Dave over there,' I indicate Dave, who just stares back blankly.

'And the other lads are the recruits we met at Salisbury. My sister is in London, I'm going to try and get her, which is why we've got the big vehicle. Didn't any of you hear that broadcast on the radio?' They look at each other in confusion, then back to me with eager faces.

'What broadcast? Has the Government released a statement?' Mark asks.

'I don't know about the Government, but I heard a broadcast on a car radio. It said that London was infected and for survivors to head to the Forts on the South Coast.'

'Well, just who put the broadcast out? Who sent it and what else did they say?' Mark says, his tone becoming more forceful.

'I don't know, it didn't say – it was just a looped message on a random frequency. Didn't any of you go through the radio frequencies?' Some shake their heads and others just stare back at me, blankly.

'Don't any of you watch the movies? In horror movies, they go through the radio frequencies and search for government messages.'

I am dumbfounded at the amount of people I have met so far that have not bothered to do this.

'I don't think any of us have scanned the radio but ... what's this about rats?'

'We were getting fuel when we saw hundreds of rats staring at us. Now this whole area is covered in them, they've got the same red eyes as the zomb ... the *strange* people have.'

'I told you Mark, that they were coming up through the toilet,' the woman who ran screaming earlier says. She too is wearing a smart business suit and has the same cultured tones as Mark.

'Yes, thank you, Cynthia,' Mark says without even looking at the woman.

'Listen, we need to secure this building and make sure they can't get in,' I say to the group.

'How will they get in?' a woman holding the child asks, her face pale and drawn.

'Rats can get in anywhere: through air vents, drains – and, with so many of them in full force, they can chew through most materials.'

'Oh my God, they'll get in and kill us … They'll kill my babies!' She starts panicking, clutching the child closer to her.

'No, we'll secure the building and figure something out. Even if it means just waiting until they go away or die.' I turn to Tom.

'Tom, we need you to explain the layout of the building to us and identify any rat entry points.'

'Okay. Now?' Tom asks.

'Yes mate … lads, gather 'round.'

'Now … just wait a minute, I think we were talking,' Mark says with a condescending tone.

'No, mate,' I say, cutting him off. 'We have to do this now, before it's too late. We can talk more later.' I make a point of turning away from him and looking at Tom.

'Is there a flat roof?' I ask Tom.

'Yes, it's quite big actually,' he replies.

'Okay, we need to get someone up there. Is there access from inside the building?'

'At the back, there's an access ladder.'

'Jamie, you've got the rifle, I want you up-top – but we need a way for you to communicate with us down here.'

'There's a couple of skylights in that central area, sir – we could open them so that Jamie can shout down,' Blowers says.

'Tom, will they open without being forced or broken?'

'You just need to undo the latches. This place is open twenty-four hours a day, seven days a week – so they're not a security issue,' Tom replies.

'Okay, good idea, Blowers. Jamie, do that then, mate – crack open one of the skylights and shout down to make sure we can hear you – every twenty minutes – so we know you're all right, got it?'

'Yes, sir,' Jamie Reese replies.

'Right, we keep two in the middle area at all times, watching the front and the rear, and then a couple on constant patrol around the building, checking all of the rooms. The rest of us will make the building secure ...Tom, does that shop stock Sellotape?'

'What?' Tom asks.

'... or brown parcel tape?' I say to him.

'Oh right, yes they do – we have to get some of our office supplies there, if we run out.'

'Right, okay, if any of you want to help, that would be great,' I look at the group seated in front of me. An old man and woman quietly look at each other.

'We'd be glad to help you, young man,' the elderly chap says.

'I'll stay here with Mary and help to look after the children,' the old woman says, indicating the scared woman clutching the child; a baby in a removable car seat sleeps next to her.

'Tucker, we need to get moving. While we start getting the building secure, you go through the supplies and see how much food and drink we have.'

'Yes, sir,' Tucker responds and shoots off towards the counter.

'Dave, can you come with me, Jamie, and Tom, to look at the roof?'

'Yes, Mr. Howie.'

We go through to the back of the building into the utility and office areas. Tom explains that they have daily deliveries, so the only stock will be what is in the shops and cafés. We stop at a metal access ladder that leads up to a small landing and a door. Tom ascends first and unlocks the door with his set of keys. We follow up and step out of the door into the bright sunshine, ready to respond, in case the roof is covered with rats. The sides of the building are sheer and, unless the zombie rats start stacking boxes, it will be unlikely that they can get up here.

'All of the wiring and pipes are underground, so there are no attachments to the building anywhere,' Tom says, as we walk around the perimeter.

The view is much worse than I thought it would be. The ground level is thick with rats, stretching out across the car park, all the way back to the still burning fuel station.

'At least now we know who caused that,' Tom says.

'Yeah, sorry about that mate – bit of a desperate situation,' I apologise, watching the thick, black smoke pluming up into the sky, sending a massive smoke signal to every undead in the area.

'We can expect more visitors now,' I say to Dave, who nods. The rats are climbing on top of each other at the edges of the building, each one desperately fighting and squirming to get inside.

They are on all sides of the building now, and hundreds more are still pouring in from all directions. We get to the central skylight and undo the clasps on the sides; the top can be fully removed, but that would be dangerous; rats might descend very quickly, like in the Saxon.

'Just crack it open a few inches so we can slam it down, if we need to,' I say.

'Cookey? Nick? Can you hear me?' I shout down.

Two faces appear underneath me, grinning up.

'Loud and clear,' Cookey shouts up.

I move away a few feet.

'How about now?' I call out.

'Yep, still good.'

I move over to the edge of the building and call out again.

'Yep, we can hear you fine,' Cookey shouts up.

'Okay, Jamie – all yours. Shout down every twenty minutes so we know you're still alive.'

'If I see any of the *people*, can I fire on them?' Jamie asks me. I look to Dave and we both nod.

'Yes, mate, but let us know first, so we don't all jump out of our skins.'

'Okay, Mr. Howie.'

Bugger, he *is* slowly turning into Dave.

Back downstairs, I see that Blowers has already divided them all into teams and sent them off into various sections to secure the building.

'I told them to tape up every possible entry point,' he says.

'Well done, mate.'

I watch as Dave walks down the aisles and stops to pick something up from the shelf. Then he walks over to the counter, to a tray of cigarette lighters. He raises a can of hairspray and presses the button as he sparks the cigarette lighter, and a long flame shoots out from the nozzle of the can – he looks over to me and smiles.

'I knew we'd have flame throwers at some point,' I jokingly groan. 'Bloody good idea though, mate, let's hand them 'round to everyone. But ... they might burn the building down ... maybe we should put them at key points, so we can spray into the drain openings and toilet bowls – in case they break through.'

Dave nods in agreement and we start walking through the building, watching the recruits and the people from Burger King taping up every air vent and drain cover. Darren Smith is stretching tape across the gap, just a few inches back from the front door.

'It won't stop them, but it might buy us a bit of time, sir,' he says, as we stop to help.

'Tom ... we need a safe, secure place we can all go to, in case they get through.'

'The storeroom or the office? The office has the cash safe in there – so it's the most secure, just very small,' he replies.

'Will we all fit in there?' I ask him.

'Probably not, so ... we could use the office *and* the storeroom – if we make the storeroom fully secure.'

'They are connected by the corridor, aren't they?' I ask him.

'Yes, so we could fall back to the storeroom first and then the office – if all else fails,' Tom replies.

We walk through to the back area; the old chap from Burger King is working with McKinney, taping up the air vent. I check the rear access, a double metal door with safety bars on the inside and thick-looking bolts on the top and bottom.

'We should keep these doors clear, they look strong, and even rats can't chew through metal quickly.'

I explain the plan to the old man and McKinney and then work with them to secure the room completely. The door leading into this area from the main building is only a single wooden door. There are some stock cages in the storeroom and I work with Dave and McKinney to pull the cage off the wooden base. Once free of the wooden base, the metal cage stretches out – it's fine mesh and we jam it against the door.

'That should hold them for a bit longer, if needed.' We remove the mesh barrier and rest it to one side. We hear shouting and run into the main area to see Nick booting a rat against the wall.

'Coming from the ladies' toilets,' he yells, and we run in to see thick, black bodies straining to lift the lids with the heavy waste bins on top. The dead rats I put in the bowls have just given them something to stand on and get leverage.

I grab a can of deodorant and a lighter and charge into the cubicle. Just as the lid lifts and two of them squirm halfway out, I ignite the spray, keeping the button pressed down, and push the flame throwers at the bodies.

The rats squeal and start thrashing; the jet of hot flame incinerates their small bodies within seconds. Remarkably, they keep trying to fight their way out rather than dropping back down into the safety of the bowl. I kick out at the flaming bodies and stamp them down onto the floor so that I can crush them underfoot. I rush out and see Dave doing the same thing, but holding the flame directly on their heads so the fur burns away. He scorches them to death amidst squealing and thrashing.

'We need someone in both toilets all of the time,' I shout out as the last of the rats is destroyed by fire and stamping.

'I'll do these ones,' McKinney offers. We go back out into the main area; Cookey and Nick Hewitt are still there, but looking in our direction with concerned faces.

'All clear for now. Cookey, can you keep watch in the men's toilets, mate? Nick ... you watch this area and the front doors,' I shout over to them.

'He'll bloody like that,' Blowers shouts from off to the side somewhere.

The Undead Day Five

'Cookey likes hanging around in the gent's bogs – don't you, Cookey?' he adds, as the lads all start sniggering from their various positions. I even hear Jamie chortling from above us on the roof.

'Get Fuc ...'

'Language, lads,' I shout out and cut Cookey off before he offends everyone in the building. Cookey grins and walks off to the toilets.

'Oi, Nick ... You got any more smokes, mate?' Cookey yells, and Nick throws him another packet. We keep walking around the inside edge of the building, checking and re-checking the access points.

Nearly all of the tape is used up; there's just a few rolls left over. The storeroom is searched, but no more tape is found. I find Tucker in the other café, the one by the services company. He is sorting through boxes of food and making piles.

'Tucker, can you get some supplies into the storeroom and office at the back? They are our fall-back points,' I say to him.

'Got it,' he responds, and starts loading boxes with bottles of water and snacks.

'Also, mate ... in your official capacity of stores man – can you get those first aid kits on sale in the shop and stack them in there too? Get some dressings and stuff to the lads as well, and make sure they've all got water and something to eat ...' Tucker nods and starts moving off.

'Oh ... and Tucker.' He turns back to face me.

'Sir?'

'Thanks mate, good job.'

He smiles and walks off and Dave stares at me again.

'What have I done now?' I ask him.

'Nothing, nothing at all, Mr. Howie.'

'It's going to be a long night, I can bloody feel it.'

'Yes, Mr. Howie, it will be.'

Chapter 13

The rats sat and waited until the numbers were strong enough to attack and be sure of a victory. The infection felt the pull of the rodents as their urge to attack and bite the resistors was pulling at them. But the infection held them and waited for more to arrive. It watched from the thousands of pairs of eyes and picked up on the scent trails from thousands of pairs of noses until sufficient were present. Then, as the one they called Howie got on top of the vehicle, they commenced the attack, pouring across the small fuel station forecourt and throwing themselves at the vehicle. Many died instantly from the giant wheels crushing them, but still they poured in, and the infection knew they would be taken now. The vehicle started moving, but the infection had planned for this, tapping into some of the memories and images from the human hosts and starting to learn basic tactics. It sent rats up onto the roof so they could attack from all directions. As the vehicle rolled under the roof, the infection pushed the bodies over the edge to drop down. Some held on, but many were thrown off as the vehicle went faster, and then the one they called Howie used a loud tool to fire metal at the rats and the station exploded. The infection felt many of the rodents scorched and blown to pieces by the massive explosions, but still it sent wave after wave of rats after them. The infection moved the rats from the top of the vehicle and made them drop down into the inside, where it could see and smell the potential hosts. But those resistors were quick and the infection failed to send in enough rats to *finish them off.* It kept the rats moving and leaping at the bodies, but the boots were too thick and the rats' small teeth were unable to penetrate. The resistors were lucky, as they had no idea how many times the rats sank their teeth into the edge of the thick leather boots before being kicked away or stamped upon.

The infection watched as one of the rats gained purchase on the front of one and started to climb up to the soft skin of the stomach, but another one struck out and killed it.

Then it got more rats inside and the potential hosts stopped the vehicle and ran into the building. The rats were urged on and whipped into a frenzy, but the resistors got inside the building. The infection sent the rats against the walls and glass and forced them to bite into anything soft enough to damage. It found pipes and access tunnels and sent the rats along and into the toilets, just as it had done so many times before, but the resistors were there again and repelled each attack, killing the rodent hosts. Through the eyes of the rats, the infection saw the huge plume of black smoke rise high into the clear, blue sky. Every host across the county stopped and stared into the sky, searching for the sign. The infection saw the thick black smoke through many human host eyes and sent those towards it, but they are too slow and the shuffling will take them too long. The infection knows that it can speed them up, but they will become weaker and unable to repair the already badly-damaged and decaying bodies.

The infection calculates this risk and allows more energy to flow. The hordes of zombie undead suddenly start forward with renewed speed and they run in staggered groups towards the smoke signal.

Chapter 14

We keep pacing around the building, checking and re-checking. More rats escape from the toilet bowls but are quickly dispatched by the flame throwers used by Cookey and McKinney. They shout to each other with a running tally, competing with the number of kills they both get. Tucker has distributed water and snacks amongst the recruits, and I keep rotating them around so they don't get bored, apart from Cookey and McKinney, who are too intent on their competition to leave their posts. The people that were already here are moving about, chatting with the recruits and making suggestions, until they all gather back in the seating area of Burger King. Dave and I join them after taking another walk about and checking each area.

'How are we going to get out?' I ask Dave quietly, away from earshot of the group. 'They are too small to take on easily, and there are fucking thousands and thousands of them now.' Even Dave seems stuck for once and looks thoughtful.

'Maybe they will die quickly, but we can't risk just waiting here, they'll bite their way through soon enough mate,' I say to him.

He doesn't respond, but just looks at me.

'There must be something we can do to reduce their numbers, or get back inside the Saxon and lock the top down.'

'We'll never get through them,' Dave says.

'Okay, what about fire? But that risks the building and us too – or we could try poison? But we don't have buckets of rat poison.' I keep making suggestions, negating each one as I think of it.

'How about electrocution? We did that at the police station.'

'There's no power here, Mr. Howie, I did think about that.'

'Okay mate, do you know what we need?' I ask him.

'What?'

'An exploding cow,' I smile at him.

'We don't have any cows here, Mr. Howie.'

'I know … it was a joke, Dave.'

'Oh, okay.'

'The grenades would be no good, we're too close to the building,' I say thoughtfully.

'They're still in the Saxon,' Dave says.

'Oh well, there's that idea gone.'

'CONTACT,' Jamie shouts from above us.

The people in Burger King all stand up and look about, terrified.

'Quick, upstairs,' I say to Dave, and we run to the access ladder in the back area and climb up onto the roof.

'What've you got, Jamie?'

I race towards the front edge where he is standing, aiming the rifle.

'Look.' Jamie points almost dead ahead and I peer out over the car park to the hordes of undead zombies running towards us.

'It's not night time and they're running … why are they running?' I shout out, alarmed.

'They're coming straight for us, sir,' Jamie says.

'Start shooting them, mate.' I run across the roof to check the other sides and I am horrified to see more of them coming across the car park. More are on the motorway and even coming across the fields behind the services building.

'Fuck me, there's loads of them.' I check my watch.

'It's about an hour to sundown, but they're running now – something has changed.'

'What's going on?' a voice shouts up through the skylight.

'Zombies, coming from all sides, and fast,' I yell down.

'But it's daylight,' the voice shouts up.

'That's what I said … Get the others up, quick as you can, but keep Cookey and McKinney in the toilets, and Hewitt on the main area beneath us.' I move back to the front and see Jamie taking aim and firing at the oncoming masses; his aim is brilliant – even from this range, and firing at moving targets – he still drops them.

'Are you getting head shots from here?' I ask, surprised as they fall down and stay down.

'No way, not from this distance and the speed they are moving at,' Jamie replies and fires again with a *cough* sound from the rifle.

'But they are staying down!'

'Are they? I haven't looked, hang on,' Jamie says and sweeps the scope back to the ones he has already shot down.

'You're right, they are staying down, not even moving,' he says.

'They must be weaker. A body shot like that wouldn't stop them, it might drop them down but they would keep coming.'

I make my SA80 assault rifle ready just as Tucker, Blowers, Curtis Graves, and Darren Smith come out onto the roof, one at a time.

'Jamie is killing them from this distance with body shots,' I say, as I take aim and hear the rest of them rack their rifles and make ready.

'Spread out to cover all sides,' Dave says.

I aim at the centre mass of a large-built, undead female who is staggering and wobbling across the car park – I fire and watch her drop as she is struck somewhere in the middle of her body. I keep watching, waiting for her to start twitching and trying to get up, but she remains completely still.

I next aim for the middle of a group and fire into them. One of them drops and is instantly trampled under the feet of the others. I hear rifles popping all around me, and the coughing noise from the

The Undead Day Five

sniper rifle held by Jamie. I keep firing and feel a deep satisfaction as they are dropped on the spot.

There are more moving fast though, and they are already halfway across the car park. The rats pay them no attention and the zombies just stagger through the black bodies, treading them down or kicking them aside as they lurch forward. Even when the human zombies drop from being shot, the rats don't try and eat them, they just keep surging forward.

'Shit, look at that lot,' Blowers calls out and I look over; he is facing the motorway and I see a densely-packed horde charging down it towards the slip road. They are really crammed together at the front and then spread out to a long tail, further down the motorway.

'There's more coming across the fields at the back, too,' Tucker shouts.

'Fuck me, they don't like us much, do they?' I shout out.

'Rats and zombies all coming for us, doesn't it just make you feel special? Jamie, can you start dropping them as they come into the access road from the motorway, mate?'

'Sir,' Jamie confirms and moves over to the corner of the building so he can cover the car park entrance to the access road and the motorway. He puts his bag down at his feet and I see it's full to the brim with boxes of bullets. I move over to the skylight and shout down:

'Get one of those people up here to help Jamie re-load the rifle magazines.'

I watch Hewitt run towards Burger King and I go back to the front and take aim. There are hundreds of zombies coming for us now, and thousands of rats. We keep firing, taking single shots, and manage to keep them back from the building, but their numbers are huge and it's only a matter of time before they get to us.

'How can I help, young man?' I turn to see the old man coming up the ladder and onto the roof.

'Can you reload a rifle magazine?' I ask him.

'I did National Service, I can't imagine it's changed very much. I might be a bit rusty but I'm sure I will soon pick it back up,' he says, with confidence.

'Dave, can you show him what to do? We need to keep Jamie firing.'

'Yes, Mr. Howie, on it now,' Dave responds, and takes the old-timer over to Jamie and shows him how to push the bullets into the magazine and stack them up on the low wall next to Jamie. We keep shooting and they keep dropping, but more are coming, and we still have the rats to deal with. We are getting good results though, and the car park and surrounding areas are soon littered with bodies.

'Here they come!' the old man shouts, as the massive horde from the motorway staggers out of the access road and spreads into the car park, running towards us. I turn and fire into them, as do Dave and Jamie.

Our shots are good.

Dave stops firing and drops down to the bag at his feet; he pulls out a black pistol and hands it to the old man.

'Can you use this?' he asks.

'Oh yes, I was a good shot a few years back,' he replies, taking the gun and examining it with steady hands.

He takes seconds to figure out how to push a magazine in and slide the top back.

'When they get closer, start using it,' Dave says simply, and goes back to firing at the massed horde charging towards us. I keep shooting into them, but the numbers are too high and they are relentless. They get halfway across the car park and the old man raises the pistol and starts firing – sharp cracks fill the air as the handgun fires and his arm hardly moves from the recoil.

He drops several of the undead with his first magazine and starts re-loading, checking to make sure Jamie has enough magazines before he continues firing.

Despite our constant firing, they reach the front of the building and slam into the glass doors with a loud bang.

'Tucker, get down and support Nick in case they get through,' I shout and Tucker runs towards the ladder. I switch the assault rifle to fully automatic and lean over to look down at the already-packed horde and squirming black bodies jumping up between them.

I then press the trigger and watch as they are cut down from the rapid fire – but thirty or so rounds last seconds and I'm re-loading and firing again.

The old man is leaning over and firing into them too.

'They're at the sides,' Blowers shouts.

'Which side?' I yell back, as I change magazines.

'Both,' he shouts back, running between the two edges and looking down.

I glance at the Saxon and the GPMG sitting dormant on the top, wishing we had it now.

'At the back, too,' Smith yells out.

'How are those doors looking?' I yell towards the skylight.

'They're holding, but they won't last if they keep coming.' It sounds like Nick shouting up.

'Tucker, get those people into the safe area and make Tom keep them there.'

'Yes, sir,' Tucker shouts, and again I go back to firing down into the increasing horde.

They are staring up at us, pale, drawn, decomposing faces that are rapidly becoming less human in appearance. The bodies pile up as we shoot them, which creates a natural obstacle for the others, but they are frenzied and claw and rake at the bodies to get to the doors. The groaning noises they emit are a lot more aggressive now and they almost sound like they are growling.

'What's got into them?' I shout out as I change magazines again.

'I don't think they like us very much,' Blowers says, as he fires his weapon down at the sides.

I look up and see more coming along the motorway and from all around. Dave suddenly runs off and slides down the ladder, heading underneath us to the shop. He returns a few minutes later with a basket full of bottles of spirits and a roll of kitchen towels.

'I'll help with those,' the old man says, and starts working with Dave to open the bottles and stuff thickly twisted kitchen rolls in the top of them. Dave steps up to the edge of the building and lights the first one; he waits for it to catch alight and launches it high into the air. It smashes on the ground in the middle of a group charging across the car park. The flammable liquid ignites, and flames shoot out as the liquid bursts away. Several of the zombies are set alight instantly and they stagger forward, but drop down within a few steps.

'They really are much weaker now,' I yell out, as the old man hands Dave a flaming bottle. Dave launches it and again it hits in the middle of a group, bursting into flames that shoot up and ignite the zombies. Dave continues with the deadly cocktails until there is a line of fire across the car park. The undead run straight through it and many are set alight and fall down within a few steps, but many more make it through and get to the front of the building.

'THE MALE TOILETS ARE GONE!' Cookey yells out, and I glance down to see him holding the door shut.

'IS THAT BECAUSE YOU BUMMED THEM ALL?' Blowers shouts, and I can't help but burst out laughing.

'YES, IS THAT A PROBLEM?' Cookey yells back.

And I snigger as I fire my weapon down into the horde again, blowing heads apart and watching the bits of skull and brain matter fly off.

The doors are getting overwhelmed now and the zombies are already several deep and growing.

'Dave, drop some straight down on them, we'll have to risk it. The building is metal and glass so we might be all right. They'll be through there any second.'

Dave leans over the lip and pulls his arm back, then he launches a bottle straight down, which explodes and bursts into flames, sending smoke straight up at us. Dave grabs another one from the old man who has lit two, and they both lean over and throw them down. The liquid flames up instantly and zombies drop like flies to lie in the flames; the rats squeal and scurry about, with more frantic movements and I see many of their bodies on fire too.

Daylight fades and turns to night, as more zombies pour across the car park towards the building. As the last of the light fades they all suddenly stop and stand perfectly still.

The Undead Day Five

'Here we go,' I mutter under my breath. 'Mind you, they can't get much worse, can they?'

They all stare up at the sky and start to roar into the night, just as they have done each dusk so far. We take advantage by shooting many down, firing into them as they roar. I suddenly feel anger building up in me and I roar back at them:

'COME ON YOU FUCKERS!'

Dave joins me and we roar with defiance at these undead things that are refusing to let us be.

Blowers and Jamie join in, even the old man shouts, and I hear the lads underneath me screaming with defiance. The adrenalin courses through my system.

You are many and we are few, but we will kill you.

We are righteous and you are evil and we will destroy you.

We roar at each other, masses of zombies and a small group in a motorway service station but, right here and now, I wouldn't change sides for anything in the world.

The undead stop roaring but we continue. We scream every bad word ever known to us at them.

Dave's drill sergeant voice is the loudest of all:

'I AM DEATH AND I COME FOR YOU!' he bellows, and it sends a tingle down my spine. I let rip with every ounce of being and scream as they charge. As one, we stop roaring. As one, we lower our weapons and aim. As one, we fire.

We cut them down as they charge towards us, weapons on fully automatic now. Jamie has ditched the sniper rifle and has taken up his assault rifle and is firing into them with deadly accuracy. They keep coming and they keep dying – as we scorch them and tear them apart with our bullets.

'DOORS!' Cookey bellows from underneath us.

'MOVE BACK,' I shout and we start moving back to the ladder and dropping down onto ground level.

'Are they all in the safe area?' I ask Cookey, as I move into the main area.

'Yes, sir – Tucker has taken them and that Tom bloke said he would keep them in there,' Cookey answers.

'Where's Tucker now?' I ask him.

'He's staying with them to make sure they don't lock us out.'

'Bloody good idea. Christ, look at that lot,' I say as I look towards the doors and see a solid press of bodies squished against them.

The pressure is so much that the ones at the front are pushed hard against the glass, and I can see the black rat bodies running between their legs and feet.

'The toilets went then?' I ask Cookey.

'Yeah, we got fucking loads though. The bodies were stacked right up, but just too many of them coming out – the doors are inward opening though, so they can't push their way out.'

'Who won the competition?'

'McKinney, the bastard,' he grins.

The rest scale down and come to join us staring at the doors, when a sudden realisation hits me.

'Fuck, the roof is probably the safest place – why don't we get them all up there, at least we can still fight back,' I spin round to Dave.

'Mate, you hold up here with Cookey and McKinney, the rest of you come with me.' I run back to the safe area and into the storeroom. Tucker is just inside, closest to the door. They all jump up and stare at me with terrified faces.

'Change of plan. We need to get everyone on the roof, as soon as possible. You have to move now,' I say to them.

'But hang on, we were told to come in here and now we have to go up there? Surely this is safer?' Mark, in the business suit, starts moaning.

'Shut up, we need to get moving now, quickly, get those children up first.' I run forward and snatch up the baby and start moving back towards the ladder.

I make Smith go up ahead of me and I climb up one-handed, holding the baby with the other arm, while the mother screams and chases me, holding the other child. I pass the baby up to Smith who takes it – like it's a bomb about to go off.

'Quickly, pass me that child now,' I say to the woman.

The Undead Day Five

'No, don't take my baby,' she screams in blind panic.

I drop down and push her to the ladder and force her up the first few rungs. She climbs up, clutching the child. I force them up quickly, apart from the old woman, who, due to her age, takes a little longer. Mark is right behind her and goes to push her up faster, causing her to slip down.

'Fucking hurry up or we'll all die, you old cow,' Mark shouts at her.

Blowers steps in quickly and punches him hard to the side of his head, causing him to smack against the wall and slide down. Blowers then stands over him, watching him intently.

'The rest of you get up quickly, this man and I will wait till last,' Blowers says through gritted teeth.

Mark stares up at him with a look of horror on his face, but stays down on the floor.

'DOORS ARE GOING,' Dave shouts from the main area.

'Blowers, get up there quickly, and you,' I shout to Blowers and point at Mark, the last ones to go up. I run back to the internal wooden door leading out into the main area and see the glass doors slowly buckling inwards, the glass cracking noisily as the pressure builds.

'Get back to the ladder and up to the roof now,' I shout and, Cookey and McKinney sprint past me. Dave and I kneel down, just a few feet from the internal door leading to the back area and the ladder.

'You next, Dave.'

'No,' Dave states.

'Fine, then we'll both stay here,' I say stubbornly, and we both raise our rifles and take aim at the doors.

'Are you going or what?' I say after a few seconds.

'Nope,' he answers.

'Okay, be like that.'

'I will, Mr. Howie.' We both watch the doors, both of us being unwilling to be the first to break away.

'They'll be through those doors any second now, Dave.'

'Yes.'

'So … you'd better get going, then.'

'You really should go, Mr. Howie – I'll cover.' The glass fractures and doors start buckling further open. I glance over to him and he looks back at me as I grin. He smiles slowly back at me.

'Ready, Dave?' I ask him, turning back to the doors.

'Yes, Mr. Howie.' The doors burst open and the zombies start pouring in. We open fire on fully automatic, cutting them down in droves and sending them back to hell.

They surge forward: zombie men, zombie women, and zombie rats.

Just as they reach us, I lean over and slam the wooden door closed and brace it with my back.

'I've got the door, you go now,' I shout at Dave pushing against the door next to me.

'Dave, I've got the door – get up that ladder now.'

'I've got the door, Mr. Howie – you go.'

'I got to the door first – so it's mine.' I shout back at him over the thumps and bangs.

'No, Mr. Howie.' He grunts, straining at the door.

'Right, I didn't want to have to do this, but you said I was in charge.'

He shoots a look at me.

'So, if I'm in charge, then I'm ordering you to get up that ladder.'

He stares at me for a moment, then:

'Okay, Mr. Howie. Move quick though. The door won't hold.'

'I know mate, now go!' I shout. He releases suddenly and sprints to the ladder and starts climbing up fast; as soon as he gets halfway up, he shouts down:

'NOW.'

'COMING,' I shout back and jump away from the door and start sprinting towards the ladder.

The door bursts open behind me and I hear them charging into the room.

During those milliseconds of running, I work out that if I grab that ladder they will be on me before I can climb up.

The Undead Day Five

Dave, or anyone else up there, won't be able to shoot down because I will be in the way. Dave will most likely drop down and try to fight them all and get killed in the process, and Dave is the strongest chance they all have for survival.

All it will take is one bite or scratch and I'm done for, and they are moving fast now. There is no way I can go for the ladder; it just can't be done.

Time slows down as I reach my hand out to grab it, then pull my arm back at the last second. I race forward into the storeroom, slamming the door behind me. I lock the door and push the bolts in at the top and bottom as I hear Dave bellowing my name and the growling of the zombies as they impact on the other side of the door. The door is solid wood and will hold for a bit, plus the door isn't that wide – so they won't be able to get that many bodies across it. But they can press in from behind and eventually the door will go. I pull the opened cage sides down across the door and pile boxes and items in front of it. Sweating and breathing hard, I step back and look round. Tucker has left some supplies down here and I smile as I realise that even during those frantic few minutes he managed to get some of the supplies up onto the roof. I sink down onto the top of some boxes and change magazines in the assault rifle. Next, I pick up a bottle of water and take a long drink before I settle down to listen to them thrashing against the door trying to get to me. I hear muffled shots; the lads must be shooting down onto the horde below. I feel numb and suddenly very alone. I know that if I had gone for the ladder, I would never have made it, but already there is doubt in my mind that maybe I could have gone for it. But they were right behind me and I only just managed to get this door closed. One bite, that's all it takes.

DAVE SCREAMS as Howie runs past the bottom of the ladder; he is at the top aiming down with his rifle, ready to drop them as Howie climbs.

But he went straight past and into the storeroom.

Dave hears the door slam shut and his mind calculates that Howie got into the room safely.

'MR. HOWIE,' he bellows and then listens.

'MR. HOWIE,' he roars again.

Still nothing.

'GET ON THOSE SIDES AND KILL THEM.' Dave turns away from the ladder and storms over to the front of the building.

The people from Burger King are huddled in the middle of the roof, cowering down, while the recruits and the old man fire down into the massed undead.

'SMITH … WATCH THAT LADDER,' Dave bellows, and starts firing down into the crowd; Howie told him he was in charge and had to go. In Dave's mind, things are black and white – right or wrong. There are leaders and there are followers. Even at the supermarket, Dave admired Howie as he reminded him strongly of some of the best officers he had served under. Hardworking, kind and considerate – but also not a fool. He was always willing to make conversation and show a genuine interest in his staff. These traits are rare in an officer, and Dave admired Howie for them.

Dave knew he had been without purpose when they attacked the supermarket that night. He'd fallen back on his years of training and natural instincts to protect the base, to protect the place that recruited and paid him. Then Howie showed up and, instead of panicking or screaming, he showed those traits even more. He'd stood next to Dave when they started to attack again.

Over the last few days, Howie has shown what a natural and strong leader he is, sticking to the primary objective – but being flexible enough to adapt and overcome whatever is in his path. Doing the right thing at the right time and doing something that the Army had never done with him – Howie encouraged has Dave to be human, to joke and to smile. And during that first battle when they charged the zombies in Boroughfare town centre, Howie didn't allow the anger to control him. He channelled it and made it work for him. He was clumsy and took unnecessary risks, but Dave could see the battle lust in his eyes and knew that Howie was a man to follow.

The Undead Day Five

Since then, Dave had protected Howie. Howie took the recruits and showed them kindness and respect and, by doing so, he became their natural leader too. He protected them during the battle to get the Saxon and knew how to get them safe before the night came, and, even after that, when most men would weep or break down, Howie took the time to check on the recruits' welfare and make sure they were all okay – then joked with Dave. Dave knows those are very special traits; he has been in countless war zones and on countless operations and can see when someone is good.

Howie is good.

Howie is his friend and his leader. To Dave, killing is a skill that comes naturally; he doesn't relish it or dream of it. Killing is just something he is able to do easily. He is small and can move quickly, and is able to coordinate his movements to achieve maximum efficiency. Only with Howie has he felt that bloodlust, that feeling of fighting alongside a fellow warrior and defeating something evil.

Dave begins to feel something he very rarely feels – and it's inside, growing and gnawing at him. The assault rifle in his hands becomes something weird and strange, something that doesn't belong to him, and he stops firing and lowers the weapon down gently, then stands still to examine this feeling inside him, trying to block it out – but it pushes up inside of him and tries to take over his mind and body.

Dave blocks it and tries to focus, but it screams inside of him, it demands to be released, and it will never go away until it is let out.

'BLOWERS!' Dave roars, his voice rising above all the noise and weapons firing.

'YOU'RE IN CHARGE!' Dave lets the feeling out.

He releases it to purge into his blood stream and pump around his heart. He closes his eyes as the pressure builds and threatens to overwhelm him. Then the feeling is in control of him and he opens his eyes and draws his knives, one in each hand with the back of the blade pressing up against his forearms. Dave looks down into the horde and leaps from the building, straight into the middle of them, as that feeling takes over completely. That feeling is anger.

Dave is angry.

I SIT in the storeroom feeling sorry for myself, sorry that I'm separated from the others. Then I think of Dave. He has the address book in his bag and I know nothing will stop him from finishing what we set out to complete. I feel bad for ordering Dave away from the door like that, but he is a special man and the recruits need him more than they need me. I can laugh and joke with them, but it's Dave that has given them the skills to survive, and he can carry on showing them and protecting them. Under Dave's tutelage the recruits will prevail, and I know my sister is in good hands with them too. They will fight together or die together, and they have already shown the commitment and camaraderie they have built up. I feel proud to have fought with them and I feel especially proud to have fought alongside Dave. I know he struggles with day-to-day living, and is unable to see irony or sarcasm and cannot work out the things people mean when they say something different. But then I think back to some of the little quips he has made and it shows that, even under the most extreme event known to mankind, people can still evolve.

The building is surrounded by rats and zombies and they all want to kill us. The lads can fight them off for a while up there, but they have proven they can wait longer than we can fire, and there seems to be an endless supply of them. But the rats and zombies are trying to get *into* the building, and are all facing inwards. Not the other way. I get to my feet, my blood starting to pound in my ears. My sister stands the best chance of survival if Dave can get to her. Those recruits stand the best chance of survival if Dave takes them, and those survivors we found here stand the best chance of survival if Dave is alive to lead the recruits.

If I can get to that GPMG I can even the odds, and even if a rat or a zombie bites me the infection won't be instant, and I can still fight through or lead them away. It's a chance worth taking, for Sarah, for the recruits, and for those people.

Dave must survive, and if that means I charge out to my certain death then I will do it. I've been lucky so far, and I admit to myself

The Undead Day Five

that is mostly down to Dave, and if he could keep a clumsy fool like me alive, he will be able to do it for them.

I draw the long bayonet from the scabbard on my belt and fix it to the end of the rifle, wishing I had my axe with me. One magazine in the rifle and then the knife on the end, and that's it to get me to the Saxon. Fuck it. I do this for Sarah, for the recruits, and for Dave, and I kick open the rear doors and burst out to find a whole load of nasty zombies on both sides.

The door had swung hard and knocked two of them off their feet.

I run forward as they immediately turn and start chasing me. I outsprint them and run down the back of the building and see more of them pressing into the sides of the building. I run out and away from the building and into the car park, then turn and drop down on one knee and fire the assault rifle into the zombies closest to me.

They drop down from each shot and I thank the Lord for whatever has made them weaker. I run on as more of them start running after me, and I see more turning away from the building, coming towards me. I turn right and start towards the front of the building, the rage and anger building inside me. I get to the corner and see the Saxon immobile a few feet from the building; hordes of zombies are facing away from it, towards the front, and surging into the open doors of the services building. I run forward, desperately trying to reach the Saxon before they see me – but the ones chasing me must send some signal or make noise because they turn and start towards me. I drop down and fire the remains of my magazine into them, tearing them apart and watching them fall and get blown backwards.

Out of bullets, I start charging towards the Saxon, roaring with anger; the top of the roof at the front of the building lights up with sustained firing, the bright muzzle flashes startling against the night sky. The recruits shoot down at the zombies as they run towards me, and I know I've been given a chance now and I take it, sprinting flat out to reach the Saxon.

Rats are scurrying around my feet and I feel bodies being crushed and kicked as I sprint over them. I reach the Saxon and race around the front to climb into the open driver's door, but there are zombies waiting for me. I charge into them as they come for me and slam the butt of the gun into the closest face.

I whip around and thrust the bayonet through the throat of the next one, as I catch a glimpse of my axe handle poking out from the edge of the Saxon. I kick the zombie away, leaving the bayonet and rifle stuck in his neck, and reach out to grab the handle. My hand closes around the shaft and I draw it towards me like an old friend. I step back with my axe, my faithful and trusty axe. I know that if I try to climb in now they will be on me, so I step to meet their charge and swipe the axe into them. The heavy blade bites into flesh and sends them slamming into the side of the vehicle. I pull back and use the blunt end to knock the next one down, and I keep going and smashing them aside as they charge at me.

Suddenly, there's a gap, and I quickly climb into the Saxon and slam the door closed. I dive over the back of the driver's seat and into the back. The rear doors are open, and an undead appears and starts clambering in with his teeth bared. I step forward and lash out with my boot, connecting to his face and pulverising his nose. Another one charges towards me, and I slam the axe down on his head, breaking his skull open. I overextend and fall out of the back doors and onto the ground. A zombie is inches away from me, bending forward as he lunges for the bite. I press backwards, up against the open rear door of the Saxon, and realise I have nowhere to go. The zombie's head then bursts apart from a round fired from an assault rifle held by someone on the roof.

That had to be either Dave or Jamie firing; either that or one of them is trying to kill me. I clamber back inside the Saxon, pull the doors closed, and move towards the ladder that leads up to the GPMG. A fat black rat drops down as I look up.

'JUST FUCK OFF,' I scream, and pick the thing up with my bare hands and launch it hard against the metal rear doors, the body exploding on impact. I climb up and see another rat on top of the machine gun and punch it full in the face, sending it flying off the side of Saxon. I rack the bolt back and spin around to the front

The Undead Day Five

of the building, and the huge horde of undead zombies charges towards me. My face splits into a grin as I pull the trigger.

DAVE DROPS DOWN into the horde, using their bodies to break his fall, and instantly he is up and spinning about. The absolute anger and rage burns through him, makes him fight faster than he ever has done before.

His arms spin and his legs kick out as he drags the deadly sharp blades across throats and slices open the arteries. He pushes forward, using the knives to puncture the backs of zombies too slow to turn, and plunges the knives into their necks. With amazing athleticism, Dave cuts through the horde, slicing them apart and tearing flesh open with each precise sweep of the blades. He roars into the night and they charge at him; he spins and ducks and leaps through them, killing them swiftly and dispatching them with gruesome finality. Two of them charge at him, and Dave drops his upper body down but raises the knives high and wide and pushes through the middle of them, slicing their necks open as he pulls the blades past him. He pulls his arms forward and thrusts the points through the necks of the next two, dropping them instantly, and he keeps driving forward, killing anything in his path.

The anger and the desperation to rescue Howie overwhelms and consumes him.

The perfect killing machine – trained only to destroy with ruthless efficiency – allows the rage to spur him on, and those skills become more deadly than ever before.

Dave fights his way into the building and down the main area, working his way through countless zombies; the bodies drop behind him as he whirls and dances through them.

Fighting and killing to get to Howie. Fighting and killing to rescue his leader and his friend. Dave reaches the door and pushes against it hard, bellowing out:

'MR. HOWIE.'

The door is locked and barricaded, and he hammers on it with brutal strength as more zombies enter into the main area behind him.

Blowers drops down from the ladder and fires into the oncoming undead, then joins Dave in beating at the door.

Between them, they force the door open and push the barricade away, bursting into the room to find Mr. Howie gone and the rear doors wide open. They charge out into the night and continue fighting their way around to the front of the building. Dave uses his knives to rip them apart and Blowers uses his bayonet and butt of the rifle to cut, slice, and slam them down. Rats pour out after them and jump at their legs as they fight and keep moving – both of them roaring and growling with ferocity and fury. Just as they reach the corner of the building the GPMG starts firing and they both turn and run out to the car park, then duck down to get to the side of the Saxon.

Mr. Howie is on the heavy machine gun, firing into the front of the building and cutting down anything that moves.

I KEEP FIRING and tearing them apart; for each one I kill, I know that I give the others a fighting chance for survival.

My mind is blazing at the destruction I am causing before me, as the bodies are ripped apart, brains and heads bursting apart and limbs being taken off.

Blood, bone, and bits of body fly everywhere and even the rats are squirming to get away from the deadly hail of bullets. I hear shouting and turn to look down at Dave and Blowers crouching by the side of the Saxon. I grin down at them and wave for them to climb in and watch as they pull the driver's door open and disappear inside.

I turn around and aim towards more undead that are coming into the car park from the access road, and together with the recruits firing from the top of the roof, we slaughter them all.

'MAGAZINE' I yell as the GPMG clicks empty.

The Undead Day Five

'LET ME DO IT,' Dave yells from below me and I drop down, grinning at him stupidly as I reach the bottom.

He grins back and there is a look of relief on his face as he stares at me.

'Where did you two come from?' I ask them.

'Dave jumped off the building and killed 'em all, to get back inside,' Blowers says.

'Fuck me, bloody hell, mate, I would have stayed there with my feet up if I'd known that.'

'Good to see you, Mr. Howie,' Dave says, as he climbs up to change the ammunition box on the GPMG.

'You too mate, and you, Blowers, did you leap off the roof too?'

'No, I came down the ladder like a normal person,' he says, grinning at me.

'I'll take over,' Dave shouts down and the machine gun starts up again. I tap him on the leg to get his attention and he stops firing.

'Is the front clear? Me and Blowers will make a run for the ladder and get back on the roof, are you okay here, Dave?'

'Yep, all clear, I'll be alright here,' he shouts, and starts firing again. We open the doors and climb out, slamming them shut again as we run towards the front of the building, jumping, clambering, and slipping on all of the broken and mashed-up bodies. The rats are still running about but they seem less directed now and slower. Many of them are dead. We get to the ladder and climb up onto the roof; the recruits are all waiting for us, smiling and cheering as we come up to them.

'Well done lads, I think we got most of them now,' I say to them.

'We? You did most of it, sir … how did you get to the Saxon?' Tucker gushes, his face red and sweating as he hands me and Blowers a bottle of water each.

'Ah you know, just sort of legged it and hoped for the best. Jamie, was it you who shot that zombie that was about to bite me?'

'Yes, sir,' he says.

'Bloody good shot, mate, well done, you saved my life.'

He blushes as the lads pat him on the back.

'How's it looking now?' I ask them and walk around the sides of the roof, looking down.

'We got nearly all of them,' Cookey says.

'Just a few left to get, and the rats of course.' Looking down from the roof, I'm amazed at the huge amounts of torn and broken bodies lying about covered in blood. The front is a mess; corpses everywhere. I look over and see Dave scanning around with the machine gun, looking for something to kill. Jamie has got the sniper rifle back and is also sweeping the whole area, the rifle giving little coughs as he fires into the night. Within a few minutes, we are relaxing with bottles of drink and munching on chocolate bars as the lads regale each other with how many kills they got.

I walk over to the central area, to the group we found in Burger King.

'Everyone okay?' I ask them.

Tom stands up and looks at me.

'So you got them all?' he asks.

'Yep, pretty much. The rats are still down there, but they are getting slower and some of them are just dying where they stand. If they keep going like that, they should all be dead by sun up and we can get rid of any that remain.'

'So … what happens now?' Tom asks me; the others all look over.

'Now? Well, we rest here for the night and move out in the morning, I guess.'

'What about us? We have lost our safety,' he says, looking down at the ground. I get the impression he has been forced to speak like this and is feeling ashamed.

'You weren't safe here for long; it was only a matter of time before they found you, or before looters came for what was left inside. When daylight comes, you should find vehicles and head for the Forts. Stick together and avoid the towns and cities and you will be okay.'

He nods and turns back to the group and they start discussing things with lowered voices. I walk away, feeling like I'm intruding on their discussion.

'You staying there, Dave?' I shout down to him.

'Yes, Mr. Howie – for a bit anyway.'

'Okay mate, we'll get someone down to take over in a bit.' I arrange for the lads to take shifts, and I do the first one.

Walking slowly around the edge of the roof and peering out into the darkness, I can't believe we came through this again. The odds were overwhelming, but we stuck together and backed each other up. I feel shocked but humbled that Dave leaped off the roof to try and rescue me, while I was charging out into a horde that size to try and keep him alive. We really must coordinate our heroic efforts next time – or this bunch could have ended up with neither of us.

We only made a few miles again today. But, tomorrow is a new day.

We have a full tank of fuel and a straight road into London. What can possibly go wrong?

IF THE INFECTION had feelings it would be feeling hurt and humiliated now. It sent wave after wave of rats against them and then many human hosts too, but the infection pushed them all too hard and weakened them. The energy needed to drive the bodies on like that during the day meant it couldn't work fast enough to prevent the injuries from shutting the bodies down. The rats slowly stop charging about as their bodies decay from within at a rate faster than the infection can fix.

They slow down, becoming harder to control, until they simply drop down and die, again. The infection watched the one called Howie and the smaller one killing the hosts again and again. The infection was sure it had them when the front doors were forced but, yet again, their cunning and guile kept them safe. But the infection learns and evolves and tomorrow is another day, another day to find and take over this group of resistors. What can possibly go wrong?

Also by RR Haywood

EXTRACTED SERIES
EXTRACTED
EXECUTED
EXTINCT

International best-selling time-travel

#1 Amazon US

#1 Amazon UK

#1 Audible US & UK

Top 3 Amazon Australia

Washington Post Best-seller

In 2061, a young scientist invents a time machine to fix a tragedy in his past. But his good intentions turn catastrophic when an early test reveals something unexpected: the end of the world.

A desperate plan is formed. Recruit three heroes, ordinary humans capable of extraordinary things, and change the future.

Safa Patel is an elite police officer, on duty when Downing Street comes under terrorist attack. As armed men storm through the breach, she dispatches them all.

'Mad' Harry Madden is a legend of the Second World War. Not only did he complete an impossible mission—to plant charges on a heavily defended submarine base—but he also escaped with his life.

Ben Ryder is just an insurance investigator. But as a young man he witnessed a gang assaulting a woman and her child. He went to their rescue, and killed all five.

Can these three heroes, extracted from their timelines at the point of death, save the world?

Printed in Great Britain
by Amazon